The Smuggler's Quest

Lily A. Bear

Christian Light Publications, Inc.
Harrisonburg, Virginia 22801

Christian Light Publications, Inc.,
Harrisonburg, Virginia 22801
© 1999 by Christian Light Publications, Inc.
All rights reserved. Published 1999
Printed in the United States of America

09 08 07 06 05 04 03 02 01 99   5 4 3 2 1

ISBN 0-87813-587-1

Contents

Introduction

When Hugo Donado took me over the slippery jungle trails he had used while smuggling contraband, when he showed me the easier river crossing through the cane fields, and when we walked with his family to the little chapel and worshiped, I sensed that God had changed this man's life. I never knew the old Hugo, only the new.

"Why do you want to share my story?" he asked.

"It's a story of what God can do," I answered. "Many youth are struggling on the same road of self and sin without Jesus Christ."

Since Hugo asked that his identity be hidden, changes have been made in this account. But we who have had the privilege of working with him know the facts have not been altered.

Miracles do happen. Jesus Christ is still Saviour and longs for all mankind to answer His call to salvation. God longs for you to be His child, and He seeks you just as He sought Hugo Donado in the jungle outback.

A special thank you to the missionaries in "San Marcos" who helped in compiling information for this account.

Lily A. Bear

Chapter 1

"Go! Get out!" Angry screams shattered the noon-hour siesta. Hugo stumbled over the doorsill of the block shanty into the oppressive glare of the tropical sun.

"Stay out! Ya hear?" shrilled Mama's high-pitched voice, her massive figure blocking the doorway. "Stay out, ya good-for-nothing sniveling cur!"

Hugo sauntered nonchalantly away from his home. Only his thin lips pressed firmly together and flashing dark eyes betrayed the hurt he felt from his stepmother's fury. But when he turned the street corner and their home was hidden behind a dense grove of palms, his narrow shoulders slumped in dejection. Kicking the dust with his bare toes, he scuffed aimlessly down the village street toward the river.

"Someday," he muttered to the palm canopy overhead offering refuge from the midday heat, "Someday," he repeated defiantly, "I will be someone big! Just wait, Mama Donado! Your eyes will almost pop out of your head when you see me,

1

Hugo Donado, handling . . ."

Hugo stopped, unable to finish his dream of greatness. What could he do? What could a puny ten-year-old do so that the villagers would some-day whisper, "That's Hugo. Know him?" Or call in passing, "What's happening?" Or be like Noel, with money to flash before his friends.

Hugo scowled, thinking of his older brother, Noel, who wore stylish clothes—new, crisp, embroidered shirts and leather boots. Mama Donado let Noel alone because he only laughed at her ranting or gave her money to be quiet.

"That's it!" Hugo slapped his leg. "I'll watch Noel. I'll learn where he goes, what he does, and how he gets his money. Tonight I will prove I am not afraid of the dark. I'll creep out so quietly that no one will know I am leaving. I will go to the river, the most dangerous place around, and come back without any fear. Then someday I will follow Noel."

Darkness came to San Marcos, Hugo's little vil-lage sandwiched between the Ramos River, a tributary of the greater Rio Hondo, and groves of dense rain forest. The sinister darkness was pushed back by blaring radios spilling music into the streets. Barking dogs fought over food scraps tossed into yards. Children laughed, running about in the shadows. Adults lounged on benches wherever a tienda hung its sign selling cold Pepsi or stronger drink. The stronger drink caused many men to stagger home after the village children had fallen asleep and night sounds had grown quiet.

Hugo cowered on his sleeping mat, afraid of the blackness pressing in on every side. Drunken laughter, wails, and curses occasionally burst forth as a fight erupted nearby.

He squeezed his eyes tight and plugged his ears. "I must go," he kept telling himself. "I must learn the night so I will be fearless." When sleep claimed the family, he rose from his mat on legs so clammy and unsteady they hardly held him upright. Shakily he edged along the wall of the cooking room, nearly stumbling over the bucket of water he had spilled that morning, causing his mama to fly into a rage.

Once he was free of the yard, he took a deep breath, released his aching jaw, and let his teeth chatter at will. He could not have told you how he got to the river. If someone had been watching his actions, they would have wondered at his sanity. Jerkily he ran several steps, fell down, gasped for breath, and looked wildly around at the foreboding darkness before plunging on and repeating the whole process.

It was good the river lay but a short distance from the village, or Hugo would have collapsed before reaching the dories tied to the riverbank. He crouched low in the first one he came to. Time seemed to stand still. Hugo felt as if he had lain in the hollowed-out-tree boat forever. He ached from head to toe. His tense muscles twitched uncontrollably. River sounds echoed across the blackness intensifying the unknown noises around him. In his mind he could see hungry alligators with beady eyes watching his dory, waiting to drown him. Or a coiling snake, ready to strike.

Minutes ticked by but nothing happened. Incoming ripples gently rocked the dory. Hugo became calmer. Bravely he ventured to open first one eye and then another. No evil pounced on him. Instead, he saw a star-studded sky glittering with thousands of pin-point lights. Hugo sat up, astonished at the sparkling ribbon of light the moon cast far down the waterway. Dark branches overhung the winding shore, but silver moonlight softened the shadows of the threatening jungle. As the wild beating of his heart subsided, Hugo felt strength flow into his body. Laughing out loud at his unreasonable terror of the darkness, he untied the dory, picked up the paddle, and steered the boat downriver.

"I have conquered fear, oh, blackness of night!" his paddle sang as he dipped it into the warm river. Each splash brought growing self-confidence until Hugo really believed he was fearless. Squaring his shoulders he steadily guided the dory midstream around the first bend and into the next where the river narrowed, throwing both sides of the jungle dangerously close together.

Shadows deepened, casting thick fingers of blackness across the water. Hugo's fearlessness evaporated. His stomach knotted into a tight fist, squeezing his breath until short gasps left him weak and trembling. A shrill screech sounded from somewhere within the jungle. To his left a large water animal slid into the river, causing the dory to dip as ripples caught the rounded boat bottom.

"Help! Help! Help!" his panic-stricken cry penetrated the fog of terror enveloping him, reminding him he was alone on the river. Somehow he managed to change position and find strength to paddle homeward. He couldn't remember tying the dory to its post or stumbling home. He only felt the safety of his mat as he threw himself across it and slept.

Chapter 2

Sunlight streamed through the Donados' open doorway. Chickens scratched for cornmeal beneath the table where Mama Donado slapped out tortillas. Expertly she dipped her fingers in water, wiped her palms, pinched off a ball of masa, and patting her hands in perfect rhythm, shaped a thin, round tortilla. A stack of finished tortillas emitted a mouth-watering aroma of toasted corn which mingled with the wood smoke.

"Ya lazy?" Mama Donado yelled, startling Hugo from his sleep. "Ain't ya going to school?" Hugo shot up, crying in pain as his sore muscles protested. Mama laughed shrilly before shuffling back to the cooking room.

Gingerly Hugo rubbed his arms and legs until the aching subsided. *I did go to the river alone!* he thought triumphantly. *And nobody knows!*

Broad daylight took the sting out of last night's frightening adventure. Hugo reveled in the knowledge that he had actually braved the foreboding alligator-infested Ramos River. In his mind he stood taller than yesterday—and stronger. Flexing his arm he gloated at the sharp pains.

Surrounded by bright sunlight, Hugo looked upon his river ride as heroic. The thought bolstered his ego, giving him confidence to dress, walk into the cooking room, help himself to a stack of tortillas, and leave for school walking like a man with a purpose.

Mama stared dumbfounded after her husband's youngest son. Normally he slunk into a room and stumbled around, irking her with his passive behavior. She couldn't abide Hugo's runtiness. Seeing the change in him left her so flustered that she never caught the jubilation on his face. Mama's shocked expression increased Hugo's self-esteem even further. *I'm not afraid of Mama Donado! I have conquered fear!* Hugo's heart sang.

From that moment on, Hugo felt a new Hugo being born, one ready to tackle anything to achieve his dream of greatness.

"You wait, Mama Donado! I will show you!" He fairly pranced to school, eager to begin learning. Hugo entered the village school well past starting time. The classroom was chaotic as usual, and no one noticed his tardiness. Few students were doing their studies. Each year, children were simply promoted to the next grade, even the nearly illiterate. District school officials demanded attendance, but little else, in the shanty villages located along the treacherous dirt roads beyond the cities.

Hugo's fellow classmates were puzzled at his unexpected studiousness. He had an air of superiority about him they couldn't understand. Their curiosity heightened Hugo's commitment and filled him with pride. He, the village shrimp, was becoming someone important!

Hugo's dream plunged him wholeheartedly into his new role. He now studied instead of loafing. He found numbers fascinating, especially problem solving. Whispers circulated through the village. "Hugo's small, but smart! Watch out for Hugo, you can't cheat him!"

"I hear I have a smart son," his father taunted one evening as he stumbled into the house. "You're dumb! Can't even cut cane. Ha! Such measly muscle!" Laughing uproariously he grabbed his son's upper arms, pinning him in a vise-like grip. Hugo stiffened as the familiar smell of alcohol washed over him. Anger burned in his heart. When his father loosened his grip, Hugo swung around to face him.

"You need help?" he asked, his voice cold and calculated. Not once did his eyes waver from his father's face. "You need help?" he asked again. "I'm not afraid to cut cane. Ask me! I'll help," he demanded.

"Okay, okay. Tomorrow," his father mumbled.

Hugo left the house as dawn stole over the jungle. He thought he was early, but before he reached the fields, the morning stillness was punctuated with the dull thuds of machetes chopping cane.

All morning he struggled to master the art of cutting cane: grab a twelve-to-fifteen foot cane with the left hand; swing the machete swiftly and surely to sever the cane just above the ground; slide the cut cane out from the tangle of other canes; and begin a cane pile.

Not a breath of air stirred beneath the towering canes. Hugo trembled with exhaustion as the oppressive heat pushed down on him, as if to smother his feeble efforts. Sometimes the stalks were so tangled that he could hardly pull them loose. Other times the lofty sticks seemed to take revenge by springing back to snap him, or snagging his shins as he worked to cut another one loose. Sheer determination to have several piles ready before the cane truck arrived kept Hugo working.

When the truck roared up the rutted trail, two piles were waiting. Hugo's father only grunted at his accomplishment, but that was gratification enough for Hugo. He knew he had done more than his father thought he could.

"I'll load yours," the driver called, swinging down from the truck where Hugo struggled to lift one of his piles.

"Your first day here?" the driver questioned as he hoisted the cane onto the truck bed.

Hugo nodded, unaware of the stark exhaustion

on his dirty, sweaty face or how fragile his small frame appeared beside the cane almost several times his height. His eyes shone like steel, challenging anyone to question his ability to work. The stubborn set of his chin caused the driver to admire his grit instead of pitying him.

"Hop on!" the driver called when his truck was loaded. "You can jump off at your village."

Gratefully Hugo climbed onto the running board. Wrapping his arms around a side post, he braced himself to keep from falling off. When they neared the village, the driver slowed, and Hugo jumped. With a roar the truck disappeared, and Hugo staggered home, washed himself, and went to school for several hours.

Morning after morning Hugo cut cane. The first days he could barely lift his machete to swing, so intense was the pain in his arms and back, but he doggedly kept on. Each afternoon when the village grew quiet, he slept, gaining strength for the next day's work. Weeks of steady cutting passed before Hugo's muscles developed and toughened.

Now he dreamed two dreams—doing something great and being strong.

Chapter 3

L ife in the Donado household was chaotic. Father Donado came and went at will. Noel followed his example, except his absences were nightly occurrences while Father's would stretch for days.

Hugo watched and waited for the right opportunity to follow Noel. Cane-cutting season came to an end, giving him back his freedom. Cane cutting had also given his wiry build powerful stamina.

One afternoon Hugo was loitering with his friends beneath the tienda's open porch. He noticed Noel and his friend Jorge nearby, standing near the telephone.

"Going to Barco?" Hugo heard Noel whisper to Jorge.

"I'm waiting for the call," Jorge answered.

"I hope it's good tonight." Noel flexed his arm muscles, unaware of Hugo's presence among the others.

So! Hugo thought to himself. *That's why they hang around here. It's where the village phone is!*

I'm going to find out what's going on!

That night Hugo kept in the shadows, watching Noel's every move. About eight o'clock a gray jeep Hugo did not recognize parked beside the bridge entrance into San Marcos.

"The only way out is across the bridge," Hugo reasoned. "They will have to either turn right to the big town of Ameca or left to Barco. Why would they go to the little village of Barco?" he puzzled. "Barco is on this side of the river, and border patrols are on the other side."

Did I hear wrong? he tossed the puzzling information around, thinking hard for a solution. *Guess I'll have to find out!* he decided. Swiftly he walked to the floating bridge connecting the village with the road beyond. Across the board planks he strode, his steps making hollow echoes whenever he stepped where an empty barrel was fastened underneath the planks. Since the river was running high, there was a slight gap between the end of the bridge and the bank where the road began. Hugo jumped across, dashed down the road, and scaled a pitch pine to find a comfortable niche in its branches. *Now I can see the intersection,* he thought smugly.

The noise of village revelry drifted across the river, cloaking Hugo with its comforting familiarity. The blare of radios, yapping dogs, and constant glow of lights helped keep the night at bay. Hugo shivered, not from the humid warmth

14

that clung to him, but from feeling alone, vulnerable to unseen dangers.

When the gray jeep crossed the bridge and turned left toward Barco, Hugo felt rewarded for his long wait.

"That's solved!" he sighed contentedly as the tail-lights disappeared. "Now back to the village to see if Noel and Jorge are gone."

"Where's Noel?" he asked several of the boys hanging around the phone.

"Who knows," one of them replied with a shrug of his shoulders.

"Ask him yourself," another challenged.

Hugo left. Taking the road home, he cut across to another street then angled back to the river. *I am going to find out when Noel returns, and why he left*, Hugo resolved.

Climbing into a dory, he waited. Before an hour was up, sleep claimed him. He was oblivious to the heavy footsteps crossing the bridge. Neither did he hear a jeep motor rumble to life at the intersection, or see Noel enter the tienda bearing a heavy load. He missed the whispered conversation and the elation Bryan and Jorge showed when they shook hands before thrusting something into their pockets.

Hugo slept, unmindful of Noel's displeasure at finding his brother's mat empty. Before pale light appeared across the eastern sky, Hugo awoke, cramped and cold. Disgusted at himself, he crept home, glad no one in the village was about. He did not want to be questioned!

"Where were you last night?" Noel hissed, shaking Hugo roughly. "Tell me. What were you doing?" he demanded.

"Where were *you*?" Hugo lashed back. "Why did you go to Barco? When did you get back?"

"A spy! My little brother's turned spy," Noel's eyes narrowed as he spat out the words.

Fury shot through Hugo. With one leap he landed on his brother, his pummeling fists catching him by surprise.

"Stop!" Noel yelled, rolling over and pinning Hugo down. But Hugo lashed back angrily. "Stop! You wildcat. Stop!" Noel jerked him up. Holding Hugo's arms behind him, he locked him into a sitting position. "Maybe I'll tell you if . . . "

"You boys, stop fighting!" Mama Donado screamed, waving her broom.

Noel laughed in her face. "No Ma'am. Got the tortillas ready? Me and Hugo need a stack; we got things to do," he slapped his brother on the back and winked.

Hugo's anger evaporated, and he sat astonished, unable to move.

"I didn't know my little brother grew up," Noel murmured, as if nothing had happened. "Where did you get so strong?" he appraised his brother's small physique. "If you are willing, I could use you." The whispered words exploded in Hugo's brain. Dumbly he nodded.

Was this really happening? Did Noel really mean it? A thrill of excitement sent Hugo turning somersaults in ecstasy.

Chapter 4

"Leo! Leee-ooo! Lee-ooo!" Mama Donado's wail of anguish wrung the hearts of the villagers gathered outside the Donado home.

"Leee-ooo!" she wailed louder and louder until her continuous screaming rendered her senseless, and she collapsed beside her husband's lifeless form.

"It's best," whispered Hugo's uncle. He and another brother carried Leo's body out to prepare it for burial.

Hugo sat hunched in a corner, watching what was going on. His passive features showed not a hint of the troubled thoughts tumbling through his brain.

Why was Mama Donado screaming when all she and Leo had done was fight? With Leo gone so much anyway, would they even miss him?

His father was dead. Electrocuted. It was a stupid death. His uncle said Leo had had just enough drink left in him from the night before to dull his awareness. Cutting jungle away from the roadway, he had carelessly chopped down a tree which toppled into a high-voltage electric line. The line snapped and became a horrible, living thing, snaking down into the brush at Leo's feet. He had struggled desperately to escape the crackling, blue-white sparks and smoke, but his dulled reflexes and the tangled undergrowth held him fast. The heavy wire slapped against his feet and legs, killing him instantly with its deadly charge.

Why hadn't his father looked before he cut down the tree? The electric lines overhead were easy to see. Anyone should have been able to tell the tree was too close. Why hadn't his father been more careful?

Did he love his father? Hugo rose from the corner contemplating that question. He guessed he did, whatever was meant by love. His father had never had any use for him, nor had he even wanted Hugo around until this year's cane-cutting season.

"At least I proved my father wrong!" he gloated to himself, thinking of his weeks of cutting cane. He hoped his father would always remember him by this past cane season. Would he remember? Hugo hoped so. Wherever his father was, surely he would still remember his family!

His uncles had his father bathed and dressed in his best clothes. Hugo was glad the clean shirt hid the mangled arm. His stomach felt queasy just remembering the charred stump. Pennies were taped to his closed eyelids to hold them down. They would be removed before the wake, but their weight would make him appear to be sleeping normally. Noel tapped him on the shoulder.

"Come help me pick out a coffin," he said. "Mama wants the best."

Several rough, unfinished coffins stood against one wall of the village wood shop. Neither boy glanced at them. If Mama wanted the best, so did they. Some coffins were varnished wood. Others had glass sides and tops.

"We'll take this one." Noel pointed to a coffin with glass sides and top. "Father will look good in it, won't he?" he asked, looking at Hugo. Hugo nodded. The coffin was handsome! Proudly the boys carried it home. Each step with the elegant coffin filled Hugo's heart with a little more self-importance. The Donado family would bury their father with class!

"Boys! The coffin! I love it!" Mama Donado threw her arms around them, shocking them with her display of affection. Noel's eyebrows shot up. Without commenting, he glanced at Hugo and shrugged indifferently.

Neighbors, friends, and relatives flocked to the Donados for the wake. Pop, coffee, and cookies were offered to each guest waiting admittance into the cooking room to pay Leo their last respects.

Soft crying, sobs, and moans filled the house

and spilled into the darkness. Periodically a close female relative burst into wild, uncontrolled weeping until she was on the verge of collapse. Two male relatives were on hand to carry the grief-stricken mourner out through the throng of waiting people. Revived in the fresh air, the mourner's hysterics subsided, and she rejoined those inside.

Around midnight the villagers returned to their own homes leaving the Donados with several friends willing to watch over their dead.

"A phone call for Noel," one of the village youth said breathlessly early the following morning. "From the States."

"Hope it's Vada!" Noel dashed down the street with Hugo at his heels. Yes! Hugo hoped so too. Would Vada come for the funeral today? Hugo hoped, but knew hoping was useless. America was too far away! Both boys pressed their ears against the receiver to hear big sister Vada's voice.

"Noel! I just got the message!" she cried. "I was gone until late last night and couldn't call till now. It's awful! I wish I could see Daddy again!" Her sobs from far away in America touched the boys. Pain squeezed Hugo's heart, and tears streamed down his cheeks. He was crying for Vada. Vada, his only sister, who sent him American gifts and thought he was still a little, weak, backward boy. Vada, the only person who had stood up for him and protected him, who took care of him as a little boy before Mama Donado came to live with them. Vada, who had been gone so long that Hugo had forgotten her in his quest to fulfill his dreams.

"I'll try to come home sometime, but don't know when that will be. Write to me, boys. Tell me about Daddy!" She started crying again. Static interrupted the connection, leaving the boys holding a dead phone.

"I wish she could come," Hugo hiccuped, trying to swallow a sob rising in his throat.

"We'll make her proud of us, you and me," Noel stated matter-of-factly. Hugo's sobs vanished. Did Noel mean it? Would Noel really do things with him?

Running the back of his hand across his face, he erased his tears. For Vada he could cry, but not for his father. After the funeral he and Noel were going to be a team! He couldn't wait!

Hugo kept thinking of what he and Noel might do. Even as they walked to the church, he pondered the future. As they entered the building, Noel and Hugo each took one of Mama's arms, and walked with her up the aisle to the front bench.

Hugo's mind teamed with questions. He couldn't wait until the burial was over to find out what Noel had in mind. Mama Donado's mournful moaning kept tempo with the priest's voice as it rose and fell while he offered words of comfort. Hugo squirmed. Would the service ever be finished?

Hugo looked around the filled church. Flowers spilled over the coffin, and the rich perfume from freshly picked purple bougainvilleas mingled with the scent of burning candles. Even the cross behind the priest had been given new purple flowers for the occasion.

He thought of Vada and what he would write to her. "Tell me about Daddy," she had said. In the polished glass coffin, Leo looked as if he were sleeping, all dressed up in his very best clothes. Even his shoes gleamed from their fresh shining. Vada would be proud if she could see him.

The service was over, and the guitarist played softly, sadly, as they carried the coffin to its newly dug grave. As Hugo's uncles lowered the coffin, Mama Donado began screaming and tried to hurl herself into the open grave. "Leo! Lee-ooo!" she cried as relatives grabbed her, pulling her back from the grave. They held on to her until the dirt was shoveled in and the flowers carefully placed on top.

That afternoon Mama Donado seemed to forget her grief as she entertained Leo's many relatives. Hugo watched in disgust as she drank freely from a bottle. Her course laughter disgusted him. "I'm never going to drink," he vowed. "Never."

Chapter 5

Contraband! Hugo lived and breathed contraband. Three years had passed since his father's burial. It had been three years since Noel took Hugo into his confidence, showing him his stash of money and how easy it was to make. All it took was muscle and smarts. Three years had added more strength to Hugo's slight frame. They had also given him insight into the smuggling network in which they were involved.

Barco, the little river village, proved a great asset to smuggling. The whole village was involved, for smuggling contraband was how people made their living. Whenever police or customs officials came, the children quickly warned of their arrival and kept silent if questioned. Barco's smuggling was no secret to other villages, but its remoteness and the villagers' loyalty to each other kept officials from arresting anyone.

Dories ferried goods across the Rio Hondo to a military base in the adjoining country. Corruption was rampant. Many of the military actually helped in the smuggling network. Even customs officials saw it as an easy way for everyone to make extra money.

"Why don't you open a store?" Vada had written soon after Leo's death.

"I'll tend it," Mama Donado had offered. "And I'll give you boys some of the profit," she had said generously. But in the three years since their tienda had opened, no sales money ever reached the boys. Noel laughed at Mama's ignorance. Sure, they supplied her legally with flour, beans, rice, and soap. They never told her having a store gave them permits which they also used to get illegal goods. In addition, they charged Mama more than they paid for her goods, but she never caught on. She loved having ready cash.

"Give her a little money and stay out of her way," Noel told Hugo when Hugo fussed about not receiving any profit from the store, "then Mama will stay off our case."

Hugo loved the challenge smuggling provided. Packing out one-hundred-pound sacks of flour through a mile of treacherous jungle was not for the fainthearted. When they used their legal permits, they made day trips through the hot, steaming jungle. Hordes of mosquitoes tormented the weary backpackers.

Three years ago Hugo had staggered under the loads, barely able to carry them over the slippery, muddy trails. After delivering his flour, he had often suffered for hours from the sharp stings received from accidentally grabbing thorn trees to keep from falling and losing his precious burden.

But three years had hardened Hugo to the discomforts and sharpened his already keen sense of hearing. He no longer staggered under his loads but could hike even the most treacherous trails.

Noel handled all the money and gave Hugo a portion. He also took care of flour orders from other shops in the larger villages. He still bullied Hugo and only wanted him around to carry goods. They worked together but were never a team.

One evening Hugo was frustrated. He hung around Noel's friends, keeping well in the shadows so that no one would know he was about. Why wouldn't Noel do anything with him? Why didn't he want him around except for work? When the work was finished, Noel invariably ordered, "Get lost! Find your own buddies!"

"Found a car yet?" one of Noel's friends asked.

"I'm looking at one!" Noel boasted. "I only need two hundred more dollars! I should have that in a couple more weeks."

Hugo seethed at Noel's boast—two hundred in a couple weeks! The idea.

"Hasn't caught on yet!" Noel's words and boisterous laughter caught Hugo's attention. *Who is he talking about?* Hugo wondered. *What does Noel mean? Who hasn't caught on?* He had a feeling Noel was talking about him. "I'll find out," he muttered, slipping soundlessly away. He knew where Noel hid his money.

"Eight hundred, nine hundred, nine hundred and seventy-five dollars!" Hugo's eyes grew wide at the wad of bills he had just counted. He knew Noel had been penniless after paying for their father's funeral. Where had he gotten all the money? Carefully he put it back into the glass jar and replaced the floorboard. He was going to watch and listen. He was going to find out what was going on!

"I wonder if Noel's been cheating. Each week we pack out ten bags of flour. He gives me eight dollars a week. Since he's older, he gets double, which is fair enough," Hugo mulled over the problem. "But he's always buying new clothes and spending money on parties and friends! It just doesn't add up! If I hadn't seen the money with my own eyes, I wouldn't believe Noel has so much!" Hugo shook his head, determined to find the answer.

In less than two weeks Hugo discovered how Noel made all his money.

"Mister Conway?" Hugo approached one of their regular buyers. "How much flour do you buy from my brother, Noel?"

Mister Conway peered over the counter at Hugo. "You taking over the business?" he questioned warily. Mister Conway didn't trust anyone. He knew Noel Donado sold more flour than his permit allowed. Mister Conway himself bought goods on the black market too. What was Noel's little brother trying to do, get them both into trouble?

Hugo never flinched under Mister Conway's gaze. "My brother and I are splitting. Do you want the best deal or no?"

Mister Conway's head tilted back as he roared with laughter. "You do mean business! You do mean business!" he laughed again, slapping the counter. "I use two bags a week." Mister Conway lowered his voice. "How much do you sell it for?"

"Depends," Hugo shot back. He hadn't the least idea what flour was selling for. If he acted as though he knew, maybe Mister Conway would tell him what he paid! "Depends how honest you are. You tell me what you pay, and I'll see if I want you as a customer before we deal," he answered shrewdly.

Mister Conway roared again, "You sure know how to do business, son! Your brother charges $8.00 a hundred pound sack."

Mister Conway watched amazement, then anger flash across Hugo's face. Conway had suspected Hugo was being taken advantage of, but he liked the lad's grit and wanted him to come out on top.

"Next week," Hugo stated each word with deliberate emphasis, "I will deliver you two bags for $7.50 each."

"A deal." Mister Conway grinned as he reached

across the counter and shook Hugo's hand firmly.

"Thank you mister." Hugo beamed triumphantly. He felt like whooping! He'd outsmart Noel yet!

"Just a minute." Mister Conway touched his arm. "Don't you need to know what I pay for beans, soap, and rice?" He winked before giving the prices. Hugo blushed, embarrassed that Conway saw through his strategy.

His next two stops were easy. "Noel and I are splitting," he informed each tienda proprietor. "I'm delivering flour for $7.50 a bag. Do you want my business or his?" Invariably the owners jumped at the chance to save fifty cents a bag, and Hugo had another customer.

Hugo's success gave him confidence to enter the biggest tienda in Ameco. He didn't know who owned this store, and he almost wavered when he was summoned to the office to talk to the owner.

"Mister." Hugo tried to stretch taller as he extended his hand. The imposing, gray-haired proprietor made him nervous. He licked his lips. "I'm Noel Donado's brother. We're, uh, splitting, and I wondered if you would be willing to buy from me." Hugo's confidence was returning. "I sell for fifty cents cheaper. Tell me how much flour you need, and I'll have it for you."

"How much can you pack out each trip?" the owner asked, sizing him up.

"Two hundred pounds," came the quick reply.

"Come." The owner took him into the back of his store. "Show me," he commanded, pointing to several hundred-pound sacks. Hugo crouched down. Swinging one sack onto his left shoulder, he reached for the other, and with equal ease, placed it on his right shoulder. Standing, he reshifted his load, walked around the room, then slid one off, then the other, to their original places.

"I do it all the time, mister." Hugo's effortless action and even breathing confirmed his words.

"So you and your brother are splitting," the owner answered thoughtfully. "How will you get my goods here? Ameco is fifteen miles from Barco."

"I'll hire someone," came Hugo's ready answer. Then he continued recklessly, "Mister, my brother's been cheating something fierce. I'm going on my own, and as soon as I save enough, I'm getting my own transportation."

This boy's a fighter, the proprietor thought. He liked Hugo's spirit. Something about him made him think of himself when he was young, fighting to own a house and store.

"Name's Victor," he told Hugo. "I'll buy from you, but why don't you start your own tienda and have other stores come buy from you for retail price? Then you don't have to deliver. Look, you are young and small. If customs officials or police see you driving and going the same road all the time, they'll be suspicious right away. Me? I'm an old man! Who bothers an old man driving a beat-up car down the road? I take different passengers; I go different times; I drive around just to be seen driving. Sometimes I stop and talk to police. Sometimes I talk with the customs officials. They come into my store. They never see me. I hire someone else to sell my goods, and they think I'm an old man with nothing to do!" He grinned smugly.

Hugo saw the wisdom of Mister Victor's advice. Already he was forming plans to begin his own business in a bigger, easier way. His eyes sparkled with eagerness. He was ready for the new challenge and couldn't wait to get home and begin.

"I'll do just that, Mister Victor. And maybe if you haven't too much to do, I could hire you to bring the goods here until I have enough money to start my own tienda?"

Mister Victor grinned again. "I figured I could count on you. Call when you need me and leave a message. I check for messages every morning."

Chapter Six

"Noel," Hugo confronted his brother, "this week's the last week I pack with you. You cheating liar!" he hissed. "I'm done working with you!"

"Little brother gets smart," Noel mocked.

"Shut up!" Hugo yelled. "Go find business somewhere else! Victor, Conway, Marcelino, and Juan are all buying from me!" he lashed out, daring Noel to interfere with his carefully laid plans.

"Buy yourself a car, go to the city, just stay out of my territory. I'll never trust you again!" he spat, hatred lacing every word.

"I'm leaving," Noel taunted. "You can smuggle in the chicken stuff. I've easier ways to make a stash! And have fun with Mama!" he jeered.

Noel left the next day without saying good-bye to either Mama or Hugo. Hugo walked the trail alone. Twice he made the trip, carrying two hundred pounds each time. Before he finished, rain began falling, turning the dusty trail into a quagmire.

Can I handle the rainy season? Is there an

easier way to get my goods? Barco is the safest, but why can't I go upriver where there is less jungle? I've heard rumors that some do. I'll check into it, but first I have to convince Mama I'm old enough to handle the store.

"Mama, we need more customers." Hugo surveyed their tiny store walled off from the rest of the cooking room. "And we need some more room." He walked around the cooking room as if in deep thought. In reality he was giving Mama time to digest the idea.

"I think," Hugo slowly weighed each word, not wanting to rush Mama, "that we could be the biggest tienda in San Marcos." Slyly he watched Mama's face for her reaction. Her eyes lit up, and Hugo knew she liked his idea.

"Did you know Noel left for good?" His question startled Mama, and her eyes shot sparks. "He cleared out this morning," Hugo continued. "He took all his clothes and is going to buy a car and live in the city." Hugo shrugged. "I've been thinking today, Mama. A bigger store would be too hard for you. I'll pay you rent for the space where the cooking room is now. We'll move the cooking room outdoors. I'll put up walls and pay you more than you make now. You'd get the same money each week. Think, Mama, how nice that would be! And I'll buy a sign, a real tienda sign!" Hugo was satisfied when Mama smiled widely. He had won!

The next day Hugo hired a neighbor to enclose

the open porch with bamboo while he scouted farther downriver in his dory for an easier place to bring goods across.

Less than a mile and a half beyond Barco, Hugo spotted what looked like an inland water spur. Raising some hanging branches, he saw that after several yards, it turned and stopped.

"Um! Someone has been using this!" A well-marked footpath led from the inland waterway, beckoning Hugh to investigate. Tying his dory, he scrambled ashore. A clear-cut footpath had been hacked through the jungle. This path was not like the treacherous streambed they used at Barco! In minutes Hugo found himself in a cane field with well-marked tire tracks leading out. Hugo hugged himself in elation at such luck. Surely his father was pleased with him. Maybe he would go to church and light some candles like Mama kept begging him to do. Mama said the candle smoke rose to paradise where Father was. He would then send them good luck if he were pleased with their remembrance of him.

Who uses this? Where do they tie their dories? Will they make trouble for me? Will Mister Victor haul this far for me? These questions needed answers. Hugo was determined to find them.

Before leaving the shelter of the waterway, Hugo paused, listening for any noise beyond. He didn't want to give this perfect landing place away. Hearing nothing, he parted the branches and rowed out into the river—right into the sight of a boy fishing on the opposite bank!

Hugo stared, his paddle motionless. The boy stared back, then waved for Hugo to come.

"Might as well find out what he wants," Hugo muttered as he rowed across the river to the boy.

"Ya looking for business?" the boy asked. "Ya new?"

"What business do you have?" Hugo answered back. "I just might be interested!"

"Come," the boy commanded. "Bring your dory in here." He lifted overhanging branches and Hugo found himself in another small inlet, this time only large enough for his dory.

I wonder how many of these are along the river? This is ideal! Hugo gazed around the hidden opening. *Maybe that is how the dories on the other side are hidden! I wonder!*

"Come," the boy called again. "I'll take you to my dad."

Hugo drove a hard bargain. Maybe he was small for his age, but no one would intimidate him! His new supplier completely changed his opinion of Hugo when they finally agreed on prices. "I thought I had an easy deal." He shook his head as Hugo left his house. "He's the first young fellow I know who understands the business as well as I do!"

A smug smile of satisfaction seemed permanently stamped on Hugo's face. He was dealing with Mister Pedro, one of the largest suppliers of contraband. He, Hugo Donado, almost sixteen years old, was now his own boss! Mister Pedro would have goods here at this new drop point. Now all he needed was pack boys for Barco. It would be great to let someone else face the risks at Barco where the illegal goods came through the military.

A week later Hugo had hired carriers and was ready to begin his own business in earnest.

"A message for Mister Victor," he told the phone operator when he dialed Ameco. "Tell him to be at the Ameco intersection tomorrow morning around 10:00. Thank you."

Three hired carriers for Barco; Victor to pick up from the new drop point; Conway, Marcelino, and Juan to get deliveries from Victor; and I've left my message with at least four other tiendas that San Marcos is the best place to get wholesale prices. And the tienda sign is up! I guess everything's ready to go! Hugo went over all the changes accomplished in the past week. It felt good, really good. Even though it took all his savings to get started, he was his own boss.

Chapter 7

"**G**ringos! Menonitas! Misioneros! Right next door!" Mama Donado's shrill voice penetrated the new cooking room and into the store.

Hugo hurried to the open door. A white pickup truck was parked in front of the neighboring house. Did it belong to the missionaries? His eyes bulged when a yellow bus turned the corner and stopped behind the truck. Curtains covering the bus windows made it impossible to see inside. Three men and a lady climbed out of the bus. It was then that Hugo noticed the white couple with a baby standing next door. Smiling, the lady called out to the arrivals, "Oh, Clara, I'm going to love my new house! Come, I'll show you." The ladies disappeared inside the house while the men toured the outside, taking special note of the open area under the house built on stilts.

Whenever Hugo looked, the house next door was bustling with activity. The men unloaded boxes from the back of the bus and hauled up buckets of water.

"Remember the two white men who came about nine months ago? Remember the services they held each night?" Hugo listened closely to his neighbors discussing the new arrivals. He faintly remembered hearing talk, but it hadn't interested him.

"The younger one is moving in," his customer continued. "His name is Jay Miller, remember? He could speak Spanish as well as you and I. And sing! Could he sing!" His customer left the store, and Hugo saw him stop at the bus. Soon everyone was smiling, talking, and shaking hands. They looked over at his store, pointed, and kept talking.

It was a little unsettling to have foreigners living so close. *What do they want in our village anyway?*

Several hours later Hugo began stacking packages of orange soap into an eye-catching pyramid against the wall. The plastic-wrapped packages of three ball-shaped bars were ideal for stacking, and Hugo wanted them to capture customers' attention. They were a good-selling item, and his price was even better then Ameco's.

"Hello!" Without turning around Hugo knew the voice came from one of the gringos.

"Hello, mister." Hugo turned to face his new customer. "May I sell you something?"

"Yes, but first let me see what you have." The white man towered above the counter, his blue eyes scanning the goods stacked along the wall and hanging from the ceiling. "I'll take a package of soap, a large bag each of flour and sugar, a bag of beans, another of rice, and six bottles of Pepsi."

"I give five cents for each Pepsi bottle you return," Hugo informed him.

"Sounds fair," the gringo smiled. His eyes were blue and friendly. "I'm Jay Miller," he continued warmly. "My wife, Ida, our daughter Janice, and I are moving into the yellow house next door. And what is your name?" he asked.

"Hugo," Hugo answered, placing the last item on the counter. "Hugo Donado."

"Glad to meet you, Hugo." Mister Miller smiled again. "I hope you will come see us soon. You have parents? Or brothers and sisters?"

"One sister lives in Chicago, and one brother. Maybe he lives in the city, maybe not." Hugo shrugged indifferently. "And Mama Donado."

"Mama!" Hugo called loudly. "Come here." He knew she had been listening at the door, eager to see their neighbors close up.

Mama shuffled in, her orange-and-red-flowered dress filling the room. Her gray hair sported an enormous red bow. Silver earrings dangled from her ears, matching the three bracelets on her wrists. *Don't trifle with me!* Her hard unsmiling eyes signaled a clear message for Jay.

"Mama Donado, this is our new neighbor, Mister Jay Miller," Hugo introduced as he tallied up the goods Mister Miller had purchased.

41

"Humphf!" Mama answered. "You really are living here?"

"Yes, Lord willing, we plan to live here," Jay replied.

"Why?"

"Because we love you," Jay answered simply. "We want to tell you about God. God made your beautiful jungle around San Marcos. He created you, and He longs for you to know Him, because He loves you too."

Mama left, shaking her head in confusion.

Love. The word mystified Hugo. *What is love? How can God love me? I don't even know who He is!*

"We are having services this Sunday at the house across the road. Come," Jay invited. "Come and learn about God."

When Sunday came, Hugo was too tired to go anywhere. Saturday had been a busy day. Pedro had informed him that extra goods were available, and Hugo hated not to make use of them. "I must get more pack boys," he determined.

The following week he easily found three more carriers for Barco. "Hugo pays well and fairly." The word got around. "If you want steady work, ask Hugo."

Three months passed. Busy months for Hugo. Prosperous months. His tienda became the biggest retail store in their village. Other proprietors from nearby villages sought him out, and Hugo stopped delivering completely. Many thought it was foolish to buy goods to stock their stores from their own country's suppliers when the same goods could be gotten on the black market for half the price. Hugo Donado's store in San Marcos became the cheapest source for wholesale goods.

"I must get a car," Hugo resolved. "I'm paying Victor too much to haul, and since I won't be going into Ameco, no one will be suspicious." Taking four hundred dollars he had saved, Hugo went to Ameco to look for a car.

An old beat-up Toyota caught Hugo's eye. "How much?" he asked the owner.

"Nine hundred."

"Nine hundred dollars for that old heap? Forget it!" Hugo walked away, not even trying to bargain.

"Mister," a small boy ran after him. "My father give you low, low price. One hundred dollars off! Come."

Hugo returned. "Six hundred," he bargained. "Six hundred is all I'll give."

"Eight hundred. This car a good car." The owner opened the door, got in, and started the Toyota. "She runs great. Tires all good too."

Hugo shook his head. "Too much. I'm going down the street."

Before he had gone far, the little boy came running back. "Mister! My father give low, low, low price. We give best deal in town. Two hundred off! Two hundred off! You our friend. We help you."

Hugo retraced his steps. "For seven hundred, I'll buy it," he said gravely, handing the owner four hundred dollars.

"Four hundred dollars!" It was the owner's turn to explode. "I said seven hundred!"

Hugo shrugged. "Four hundred now, and every three weeks I'll pay you another hundred till it's paid off. If I don't pay all of it in nine weeks, I will give you eight hundred for the car."

"All right," the owner agreed grudgingly.

Hugo inserted the key into the car's ignition and started the engine. He put it into reverse and backed out into the street. Gears grinding, he found second, lurched forward, and roared off in a trail of black smoke.

Reaching an intersection, Hugo hit the brakes. The car sputtered and died completely. Restarting it, he floored the gas pedal, sending the car jerking and leaping. Hugo clutched the wheel, trying desperately to control it. He lurched around a vegetable stand projecting into the street, between two parked cars, through a row of waddling ducks, and narrowly missed a little boy who darted out to see what was going on. Hugo bounced over Ameco's exit speed bumps, relieved to be leaving town without a serious catastrophe. Maybe now he could get control of the monster! Seeing no other vehicles on the road, Hugo relaxed. Now he could practice what he had learned, watching Victor drive. He stopped the

Toyota and practiced shifting until he could easily move from one gear to the next.

Next, he worked on starting without making the Toyota leap like a jack rabbit. Mastering that, he put it gingerly into first, engaged the clutch, and sped off to San Marcos. During the twenty-five-minute drive home, he learned to take corners smoothly by easing up on the gas and then accelerating again. As he approached the San Marcos bridge, he was feeling confident in his driving skill. But the bridge was several inches higher than the roadway, and the Toyota jolted sharply when its wheels hit the bridge, sending Hugo into a panic. Instead of pressing the brake, he hit the gas pedal and the car fairly leaped over the bridge, bounced onto the rutted road, and stalled in a cloud of dust. Red-faced, he restarted the engine and chugged homeward in first gear.

"Whose car you driving?" Mama Donado yelled as Hugo pulled in front of the house. "You think you can buy something like that without me saying? Wherever you got it, take it back!" she screamed. "Now! Ya hear? You, you . . . " she stopped as Hugo walked toward her, his face impassive, and his eyes never leaving her face.

"It's my car, Mama," he clipped each word crisply. "I bought it. And don't you ever tell me again what I can or cannot do. I pay you good wages. You fuss, and I'll clear out. Then you'll have no one."

Mama dropped her gaze and scuttled back inside muttering, "Keep your car, keep your car."

It was Hugo's last run-in with Mama. From that day on, Mama let him alone, even sticking up for him to others. Someday she would even be Hugo's protector.

Chapter 8

Ominous black clouds hung heavily over the countryside, hiding the rising moon and night stars. Hugo started his Toyota, hesitant to leave the safety of the house. He couldn't shake a premonition of danger. Should he turn back? Were customs officials on patrol? Would they find his hidden boat? With border patrolling heavier, was it safe to go?

Nearing his turnoff at the cane field, Hugo shut off his lights and crept slowly past. Nothing seemed abnormal, yet Hugo hesitated. Instead of turning off at his usual crossing, he drove about a quarter of a mile beyond. Turning around, he retraced his route. Just before reaching the cane field, the moon broke through, flooding the countryside with silver light. Midway along the lane, a gleam of metal warned him there was indeed danger afoot.

Pressing the gas pedal to the floor, Hugo careened homeward as fast as he felt safe to go without lights. He glanced back to see if lights were following, but saw nothing. Heart hammering, Hugo roared down the road, thankful he knew every dip and curve with his eyes shut. Reaching the San Marcos bridge, he flew across, unmindful of the jolt that sent his head crashing against the roof. Skidding around the last corner, he cut off the engine and coasted to the side door by the kitchen. Grabbing his keys, he let himself into the house. After locking the house door securely, he entered the tienda. His sleeping mat lay beside the doorway where he slept each night to guard the store. He lay down on his mat, listening. In minutes a vehicle crept by, its motor growing fainter as it circled through the village, then left. Hugo peered out the window. All seemed quiet.

Hugo waited two hours before slipping back to the Ramos River. No vehicles were in sight anywhere, so he returned to his Toyota. Instead of starting it, he put it in neutral and pushed it to the corner. Only then did he slide into the driver's seat and start the motor. He left the village, driving without lights all the way to his second crossing. Reaching the cane field, he hid the Toyota beneath a canopy of palms. It didn't take him long to row across the river to Pedro's rendezvous hut.

Hugo rapped three times on the door, his signal to whoever was inside. The door burst open, and Pedro's middleman grunted. "I gave up on you; where ya been?"

"Patrols," Hugo shrugged. "Let's go."

It took them fifteen minutes to load the boat. Hugo recrossed the river and in a half hour had his car loaded and the boat hidden. For the second time that night he returned home without lights. When he reached his street corner, he cut the engine and once more coasted home. Noiselessly he unloaded the car, working like a shadow, nothing betraying his presence. Mama was asleep at the other end of the house. A thick grove of palms and a cornstalk fence separated him from the neighbors on the right. And on the other side, his store hid the jeep from the Millers. Across the road there was nothing but the Millers' chapel with purple bougainvillea vines climbing its walls.

Hugo grinned as he deposited the last load in his storage room. It had been a good night after all. He would have to light those candles at church tomorrow. Someone was watching out for him, and he had put it off too long already. Was his father pleased with him? It seemed so. Those were his last thoughts as he fell asleep.

Hugo awoke to bright mid-morning sunshine. Beautiful, harmonious singing was floating from the Millers' thatched-roof chapel. The unfamiliar words caught his attention, and he joined several curious villagers in the chapel doorway.

We should never be discouraged:
Take it to the Lord in prayer;
Can we find a friend so faithful,

Who will all our sorrows share?
Jesus knows our ev'ry weakness:
Take it to the Lord in prayer.

Mister Jay and his wife sang together as they stood in front of four village children seated on chairs. Warm smiles radiated from their faces, drawing the crowd of adults nearer. Hugo found himself just as interested, wondering what they were planning to do next. Their singing was unlike any he had heard. Without guitar accompaniment, Mister Jay and Miss Ida sang beautifully together.

"Boys and girls," Jay said as he paused to smile at his four eager listeners, "this morning I will tell you a story of the best-loved and most-hated man who ever lived." Jay spread a cloth with a brightly painted scene of sky and hills over a wooden stand placed before the children.

"Many, many years ago, before you or your parents or grandparents or their grandparents lived, a baby was born." Jay stuck a picture of a thatched building on the scene. Next he added a manger filled with straw. On this he placed a baby. Beside the baby he put a colorfully dressed man and woman.

His listeners were enthralled by the vivid picture. "The mother's name was Mary; the father, Joseph; and the baby, Jesus," Jay continued. Hugo lost interest in the story but took the opportunity to scrutinize his new neighbors. Miss Ida wore the same white scarf on her head he had seen her wear every day since they arrived, and her dress was no different than those she normally wore. He would have to ask Mama again what she had said right after the Millers came about how Miss Ida dressed.

Suddenly Hugo felt hot and weary. Returning home he hung up his hammock, made himself comfortable, and fell asleep to confusing dreams of border patrols arresting Mister Jay because he let Hugo sing in their chapel.

Hugo awoke, feeling dizzy and thickheaded.

"What's ya problem?" Mama asked, chuckling as Hugo stumbled and sent a chair crashing into an unsuspecting rooster. Raucous squawks rent the sultry air.

"My head hurts," Hugo mumbled.

Slyly, Mama uncorked a bottle and poured some of its contents into a cup.

"Take this," she ordered.

Hugo obediently reached for the cup and swallowed a mouthful. He gasped and sputtered, his eyes watering as the fiery alcohol burned his throat.

Mama collapsed in laughter. "Your first beer!" she hooted, rocking back and forth. "Little Hugo can't handle his first beer!"

Stung by her ridicule, Hugo grabbed the cup, and gulped down its detestable contents.

Slamming the empty cup onto the table, he left the house, jumped into his car, and headed for Ameco. Halfway there his head cleared, and Hugo reconsidered how he felt about drinking.

"Guess I'll drink some, but not too much," he said. He thought of the many times he had politely declined the beer Pedro's men offered him. Each time one was handed to him, he saw his father's lifeless body, dead because of drink. "I hate the stuff! But if it makes me more of a man, I'll drink it!" he shouted to no one. His words were swept out the open window with the rushing air. "Maybe I do need a beer now and then! I've got my own business and ten pack boys working under me. I've got a car and will be eighteen in a month. Maybe a beer now and then will be good for me. Who knows! It sure cleared my headache!" He looked in his rearview mirror and laughed. His own reflection mocked him.

Hugo roared into Ameco, hoping to find Louis, one of Pedro's men. He wanted to prove to someone other than Mama that he was a man who could enjoy a beer.

Chapter 9

Hugo shifted from one foot to the next as he watched the street. *Where are the girls?* he wondered. His fingertips drummed the counter. The clock showed five minutes to nine, the time he locked up. But where were Rosa and Elena? Weren't they coming for Cokes again? When no one came, he frowned, and locked the store for the night.

For three nights the two sisters had come just before closing time and bought Cokes. They had seemed in no hurry to leave.

"You can go ahead and lock," Rosa had laughed gaily. "We can drink our Cokes here and leave through your kitchen!" That evening had been fun. Hugo enjoyed the girls' flirting and that they chose to be with him rather than with others in the village.

"I don't like those girls!" Mama yelled after they left the third consecutive night.

Hugo shrugged; he didn't care what Mama said. Elena was sort of cute even if all she did was giggle. Hugo liked being noticed. Maybe he felt restless because he needed a girl.

I guess I'll ask Elena's parents if I can visit her!
With that decided, he immediately set out to find
her parents.

"Hello, Mister Vega," Hugo said politely after
he reached her house. "Could I talk to Elena?"

"Elena!" her father bellowed. Elena didn't
appear but her mother did, and Hugo greeted her.

"The girls are out," she apologized. "But they
will probably be back soon."

"Um, do you care if I come, I mean; I, . . . would
it be okay if . . . if I came to see Elena?" he stammered nervously, clearing his throat.

Elena's mother beamed, putting him at ease.
Before her husband could answer, she nodded
graciously. "Oh, yes! Elena would like that! My
husband would be glad for you to come too." She
looked at him, and Mister Vega grunted his consent. Hugo left, whistling softly at his good
fortune.

The Vegas grinned broadly to each other as
Hugo disappeared from sight. Hugo Donado was a
good catch, and they were proud to have him come
see one of their daughters. They would have pre-
ferred if Hugo had asked Rosa, their eldest, but if
he was interested in Elena, that was all right too.

Inside the Vegas' house, both girls watched and
listened as Hugo talked to their parents. Elena
hugged herself in ecstasy while Rosa scowled
darkly. Before Hugo had even left the house, Rosa

was hurrying to the Donados'.

"Miss Donado," she gushed sweetly when Hugo's mother came to the door. "A terrible thing has happened! Hugo thinks he loves my sister Elena, but he doesn't even know her. She gets, uh, mad every time things don't go her way, and she sneaks out to see other boys my parents don't even know," Rosa lied. "I hate to, uh, tell you this, but I don't go along with my sister, and . . . uh, Hugo is too nice for her." Rosa lowered her eyes hoping to gain Miss Donado's sympathy. "I wanted you to know."

"Wait till I see that boy!" Mama screamed, shaking her fist.

"No!" Rosa's voice rose in panic. "You musn't talk to Hugo; you must tell my parents they can't allow this. Tell them . . ." Rosa stopped, not really knowing what to say. "Tell them she's too young. I must go." Rosa darted a quick glance down the road and left.

"She's right—Hugo's too good for the likes of either of them," Mama sputtered. She wasted no time telling Hugo of Rosa's visit when he returned. "Leave them both alone," she finished, her voice neither angry nor upset. For once Hugo didn't know what to say. He was unaccustomed to Mama paying any attention to him unless she was mad about something. Perhaps he should forget the girls.

The next day all thoughts of Elena and Rosa

were forgotten. Louis announced that Pedro had invited him to a party. "You'll meet the big shots. Wear a knife; sometimes the drinking turns into fighting."

Saturday night Hugo closed early and dressed with care for the party. His embroidered white shirt was set off with black pants and shiny black boots. Critically he surveyed himself. "Too short; too small," he muttered. Flexing his muscular arms, his confidence returned. He could take care of himself! As an extra measure of safety, he took his knife as Louis suggested. He had a feeling tonight might prove invaluable to his business.

I'll drink just enough to be accepted, he determined as he neared Barco crossing. *No one or nothing will make me miss what I plan to gain tonight.*

Hugo was the youngest man at Pedro's party, but Pedro seemed happy to see him.

"If you ever need a good man, Hugo is my best." Pedro winked, clapping him on the back as he introduced him to others. Pedro moved among his guests, making sure they helped themselves to the food and drinks. Bright, colored lights were strung above the courtyard where chairs were scattered about and several girls kept the food tables well supplied. Spicy fish-filled panades; tortillas garnished with beans, cheese, and a mouth-watering sauce; steaming tamales wrapped in cornhusks; a tub filled with ice and drinks; and plates of sliced papaya and fresh limes all kept Pedro's guests happy.

Hugo found a corner near the food table where he could watch and listen. Three musicians played lively tunes on their guitars, circling among the guests, keeping the atmosphere light.

"I want you to meet someone." Louis sat down on a chair beside Hugo. "It's the heavy, middle-aged man coming towards us now," he said quietly, without looking up.

"Mister Alen Franco!" Louis rose, clapping him on the back. "Meet a new client. He may be the one you're looking for." Louis disappeared into the crowd, leaving Alen and Hugo alone.

"I've heard you are a good worker, have a good tienda, and are dependable," Alen challenged Hugo.

Hugo returned his steady gaze. "Maybe," he shrugged modestly.

Alen roared, his whole body shaking with laughter. He slapped Hugo on the back and wiped his eyes. "I've been wanting to meet you. You're fine, just fine! Now maybe you want to do business with me?"

"That depends," retorted Hugo.

Alen broke into laughter again. "A shrewd one! Ahh! I like, I like!"

Alen sat down beside Hugo and told him, "I own the biggest store in La Crucas but that is not what I want," he smiled, his white teeth gleaming in the colored lighting. "I have connections for bigger things like electronics, but I need someone very dependable."

Hugo's thoughts raced. Could he trust Alen? What about his own store? It was doing very well. He would need to think about this first; there was just too much involved to make a quick decision.

"I will consider this," Hugo answered gravely. "I have ten packers working for me now and all I can handle." He was proud to tell this man of his success. "But I will think about it."

"Good!" Alen was satisfied with Hugo's answer. "I will wait. Whenever you are ready, come to me, and we will start a big business!" Laughing at his own joke, he rose to fill his empty plate.

"Carmen," he called to a slight girl bringing more tortillas to the table. She blushed as she caught sight of Hugo but came obediently to Alen. "Bring us each a beer," he commanded.

Returning quickly, she handed one to each of them, and Alen grinned broadly. "My daughter Carmen," he explained to Hugo as he dismissed her. Hugo only caught a glimpse of her, but liked what he saw. She was slim and graceful. A mass of wavy hair framed her oval face and dark, luminous eyes.

Gone completely were any thoughts of Elena. Carmen outshone any girl he had ever seen. For the rest of the evening, Hugo was content to stay in the shadows and watch. Carmen seemed to notice Hugo too, for several times their eyes met and Hugo was rewarded with a slight smile.

The later it got, the wilder the party became. After not seeing Carmen and Alen for a while, Hugo asked another server where they were.

"They left. Her father never lets her stay very late," she answered. "He probably took her home."

Hugo left too. He didn't care what else the evening held; he had gained enough. Besides, he didn't want to get involved in the drunken brawls that were sure to erupt before the night was over.

Chapter 10

"How are you? We hardly see you anymore." Jay Miller stopped Hugo outside his store. "We miss seeing you around."

"Mister Jay!" Hugo's eyes shone brightly. "Tomorrow I am getting married!"

"Well, this certainly is a surprise!" Jay replied after a moment of stunned silence. "I should congratulate you; it's just that I didn't suspect anything. Tell me about your wife-to-be."

"Carmen is the prettiest girl from any village or city around!" Hugo said proudly. "We are going to live here with Mama, so you will get to meet her. Come tomorrow night when I give a big party for Carmen," he urged.

"We will be glad to meet her. I know Ida will love to meet your pretty wife. But remember to bring her to our house too." Jay's words held such warmth and welcome that Hugo felt a special liking for his white neighbor.

"Ida and I wondered where you have been lately," Jay continued. "We've come over different times, but your mama doesn't give any information!" he chuckled.

"Carmen's sixteen tomorrow so we can get married," Hugo explained. "Her parents said she couldn't marry until she's sixteen, so for three months I went to see her every night at seven. I think her parents are glad she is now sixteen!"

"How old are you?" Jay asked.

"Eighteen."

"Well, Hugo, you are undertaking one of the most important steps in life. Tomorrow you will be a married man with a wife to care for and to love for as long as you both live. Remember, Hugo, to put your wife before yourself and to love her always as you do today. If you ever have questions or want to talk to someone, I'll be glad to listen and help if I can. God bless you both," Jay added sincerely.

"Thanks, Mister Jay," Hugo replied, pondering the strange words. "Always love Carmen," Jay had said. He remembered when he wondered what the word meant, but not since seeing Carmen! Carmen was all love. She made him happy, and he didn't feel uneasy anymore. Why did Jay say to love her always? That would be so easy to do! He had lots of money, and tomorrow he would prove to everyone how much he loved Carmen. He would put on the biggest party San Marcos had ever seen!

The next evening Jay and Ida joined the villagers as they gathered at the Donados' for Carmen and Hugo's party. They never knew the shy, backwards, ten-year-old Hugo. They never knew the young Hugo mistreated by his mother and struggling to make a name for himself and fulfill his dreams. The Hugo they knew was either hard at work in his store or standing alone outside the chapel listening to their services. Whenever they met him, his lonely eyes and serious expression stirred in them a longing to help this youth who kept so much to himself.

Today Hugo's face beamed proudly as he presented his lovely wife to his neighbors. Mama Donado was equally proud. Her son exceeded all other village youth, and now her daughter-in-law was by far the prettiest. Hugo was sure there was nothing else he wanted. His boyhood dreams had come true, far exceeding what he had ever dreamed possible.

"Carmen is still a child," Ida said as she and Jay left the Donados'. "She seems so fragile. I do hope Hugo is good to her. And I hope she will let me be a friend."

"Hugo attracts me," Jay confessed. "He seems so intense about everything he does. I'm praying that someday he will seek to know the Lord with the same intensity he pursues his work."

That night while the villagers celebrated Hugo and Carmen's wedding with dancing, music, and drinking, the Millers were on their knees in prayer, entreating the Lord for the souls of their neighbors whom they were learning to love.

Chapter 11

Where are the rains? Why haven't they come? the villagers worried as the Ramos River dropped lower and lower. Eventually the barrels that supported the floating bridge barely touched the water. The wooden planks rested on the riverbanks, now high above the water level. Alligators sunned themselves alongside marooned dories resting on hard-baked mud. Safe drinking water became scarce as the village cisterns went dry one by one. Next year's cane fields cried for moisture. Newly planted cornfields struggled to survive under the scorching midday sun. Starving, rabid dogs with matted hair stretched over their taut bodies haunted the village. Alarm spread from one household to the next as the men feared to work among the madness sweeping the jungle.

When money became scarce, Hugo gave credit to his customers until his own stash was depleted. Gasoline prices jumped, making it almost impossible to use vehicles.

Ida Miller was bitten by a malaria-infected

mosquito. When she continued to weaken, Jay made plans to take his wife and daughter back to the United States.

"Would you watch our house?" Jay asked as he handed the house key to Hugo. "The doctor says I have to take Ida to the U.S. if I want her to live," his voice broke, weariness etched in every word. "But Lord willing, we will be back." Jay managed to smile. "God has every detail in our lives under control, and if He wills, Ida will soon recover." His own words strengthened him, and he bid his neighbors good-bye, leaving Hugo once again to puzzle over his strange words.

That evening Hugo and Carmen moved into the Millers' house to watch it for them. Living in a white man's house with its strange furnishings frightened Carmen. For the first few days she refused to stay in the house alone. When Hugo left to open his tienda, Carmen followed, spending the day with Mama Donado. But by the end of the week, Carmen was captivated by her new surroundings. She loved Miss Ida's furniture, the curtains at the windows, and the pretty pictures. Each framed picture had different sayings, and Carmen found herself drawn to the words. "Behold, God is my salvation; I will trust, and not be afraid" (Isaiah 12:2). Another read, "But as for me and my house, we will serve the LORD" (Joshua 24:15).

What did words mean? Why did they draw her

back again and again when she had already read them? Every morning Carmen read the framed words. Every evening they drew her like a magnet. *And not be afraid. And not be afraid . . .*

The words sounded comforting, but Carmen couldn't grasp their meanings. She was always afraid. She was afraid of Mama Donado. She was afraid when Hugo left at night and didn't return until the early morning hours. She was afraid of Hugo's anger when he came home demanding something to eat immediately. But especially she was afraid of his silences when he withdrew into himself and shut her away. She was afraid when she smelled alcohol on his breath.

Hugo yelled at her, but had never hit her. How long would it be until he took his anger out on her by beating her as her own father beat her mother? Carmen trembled with fear. Besides, she had a secret she was too afraid to share with her husband.

The longer the dry season continued, the more sullen Hugo became. Then one night Hugo never came home. Carmen woke from a night of fitful sleep, her dark eyes dull with weariness. Dutifully she mixed the day's supply of tortillas and put the rice on Ida's two-burner propane stove to simmer. Her hands trembled as nausea wracked her body.

It was time to open the store, but Carmen had no strength to leave the house. It could stay closed all day for all she cared.

By mid-morning she drifted into a troubled sleep, unaware of Hugo climbing the outdoor steps and entering the silent house.

Where is Carmen? He noticed the pot of steaming rice kept warm by the stove's pilot light. Beside the stove was a bowl of tortilla balls ready to pat out and fry. He found his wife fast asleep in bed, curled in a ball, her hair damp and matted. Across her forehead were beads of perspiration. *Remember, Hugo, to put your wife before yourself. Always love her as you do today.* He could hear Mister Jay's admonition the day before he got married. Funny he hadn't thought of it again. Carmen turned, moaning in her sleep.

New love for his wife surged through Hugo. He would take care of her. He had been too busy with the store. Now that would be in the past. He couldn't wait for Carmen to awake so he could tell her he was finally quitting the store to begin handling electronics which brought in big money. Last night he had seen Carmen's father, Alen, and promised to do business with him. He also promised to go into partnership with his uncle George hauling corn for the tortilla factory in Ameco.

Remorseful, he watched his wife. He had seen her so little! Money had been scarce. But now all that would change. Gently he shook her awake, eager to tell her his plans. He was ready to begin smuggling contraband in a big way.

Three times a week Hugo and George brought out twenty sacks of corn or flour. The twenty sacks equaled one ton. Before long they needed a larger permit due to increased demand.

Money was still tight, but Hugo made contacts with Zang, a rich Hindu Alen had told him about. Zang willingly loaned Hugo all the money he needed. He also helped him get a larger permit. Now Hugo and George could legally bring over fifty sacks a week from the neighboring country.

After meeting Zang, Hugo changed his name to Lopez. It made him feel safer. No one from San Marcos would know who Lopez was.

Hugo was already familiar with the border guards and used their friendship to his advantage. They willingly bought groceries for Hugo, and he just as readily let them make a profit on the illegal goods. They looked the other way when Hugo and George used the same permit over and over. They only asked for the receipt of one lot of goods per week. The guards were making money; Zang was making money; Hugo and George were making money; factory owners were making money. Everyone was happy, so no one made trouble.

Seven months after Hugo began partnership with his uncle, he became the proud father of tiny Kevin. Kevin weighed only three-and-one-half pounds at birth and needed to stay in the hospital for five weeks. Carmen went home alone, needing those five weeks to regain her own strength.

Those were lonely weeks for Carmen. Hugo's resolve to spend more time at home had lasted several days before he once again became a slave to his work. Carmen became even more fearful as Hugo's anger erupted over trivial incidents. Her fear kept her housebound because she never knew when her husband would arrive and demand a meal. She dreaded his explosive anger when the food wasn't fixed. It was easier to stay home and keep him pacified than face his anger.

Before Kevin was released from the hospital, Hugo began frequenting Pedro's parties. "Why not stay and dance and drink?" he muttered in disgust. "My wife's sick, hospital bills are large, and I need all the contacts I can make. I can handle the drink too," Hugo thought smugly as he yielded to the swinging, pulsating music.

He became a regular. And his reputation spread. *If you need a dependable man, get Lopez. Lopez will do deliveries for less. Trust Lopez; he won't cheat you. Watch out for Lopez; you can't cross him. He's smart. He holds his own.* Lopez became known as the top smuggler. While Hugo was proud of that, he didn't relax, but drove himself relentlessly. He, too, had a fear. His was not the fear Carmen experienced, but fear of the future, of failure, of someday getting caught.

Chapter 12

"**S**upper! Where's supper?" Hugo roared, as he stumbled through the door partially drunk.

Quickly Carmen slapped out a tortilla and flipped it onto the warming frying pan. Shrinking against the wall, she tried to make herself as small as possible.

Hugo's commotion startled his sleeping son who woke with a wail. Carmen glanced nervously toward the bedroom, but kept on shaping tortillas. Her eyes darted back and forth from her husband to the bedroom where Kevin's wails became louder and more persistent. Frantically she poured a cup of scalding coffee, spilling some on her arm in her panic. Grabbing the pan of hot rice she slid it onto the table along with the finished tortillas.

Carmen's frustration mounted. Kevin's screams unnerved her as she hurriedly fixed a bottle of milk. Her husband offered no help nor recognition. She loathed his wild, unkempt appearance.

As Carmen hurried past, Hugo grabbed her

burnt arm. She screamed in pain as his fingers ripped away the burned skin. Laughing at her distress, Hugo held her tighter. Something snapped inside Carmen. With lightning quickness, she swung her free fist directly into her husband's face, smashing his lips and nose. Her surprise attack stunned Hugo, sobering him enough to let her go.

Tears streamed down Carmen's face as she fed Kevin. She hated Hugo when he acted this way. She was going to leave and go back to her mother. The thought calmed Carmen. Now she had a purpose. She would not put up with anymore of Hugo's insulting behavior.

Her eyes rested on the familiar picture in the bedroom. *God is my salvation. I will trust, and not be afraid. God is my salvation. God is my salvation.* Over and over she repeated the words to herself.

"God is my salvation. I will trust, and not be afraid," Carmen's whispered words carried clearly to the kitchen where Hugo sat at the table. His food untouched, he rested his throbbing head in his hands. His lips smarted from his wife's attack. Carmen's words penetrated his foggy brain, sobering him further. All he could see was Mister Jay. Every word Jay had said seared him like an iron.

God loves you. I'm here to teach you about God. Take it to the Lord in prayer. Love your wife, remember, love your wife. Lord willing, we will be back. God has every detail of our lives under control.

Hugo pushed back his chair from the table and went to Jay's bookshelf. "Read any of our books, Hugo," Jay encouraged before leaving. "Here is the Bible in Spanish, and also several study guides that explain God's Word."

Hugo picked up Jay's Bible and another book called *Doctrines of the Bible.* Quietly he left the house, going to the hammock below. He hated himself, hated himself for drinking, hated himself for being a coward and going with Pedro's crowd. He had vowed never to drink, and here he was drunk. He despised himself. If he continued, he would either end up like his father, killed in some drunken accident, or he would end up like Mama Donado. He hated her for giving him the first drink. He hated her for taunting him, hated her for being tipsy every day, and for living with the bottle. Hugo felt consumed by hatred. His stomach rolled and pitched in revulsion. Leaving the hammock he hurried behind the washhouse and retched. He wished Mister Jay were back; maybe he could help.

"Carmen!"

"Raquel!" The women's glad cries reached Hugo at the washhouse. He couldn't see the two women as they fell into each other's arms in the doorway. Neither could he hear Raquel's soft voice exclaiming, "My dear sister-in-law," as she held Carmen at arm's length, noting her unhappiness, her burned arm, and her tension. "My dear sister-in-law," she repeated, causing Carmen to break into tears.

Raquel held Carmen as a child holding an injured puppy, and let her cry until she grew calm. "Now let me hold your precious baby boy." Raquel smiled, taking Kevin from her arms.

"He's a miracle from God. Oh, Carmen, you are richly blessed." She cuddled the baby, kissing his velvet cheeks and touching his long lashes and silky black hair. "I haven't seen you since your wedding. So much has happened. So much has changed—my life, my home, my church. I hardly know where to begin!"

"What do you mean?" Carmen asked. "What's happened? Do you mean you no longer go to the Catholic church?"

"I'm a Christian, a believer in Jesus Christ," Raquel explained. "And Carmen, I am so happy in here!" Raquel covered her heart with her hand. "In here, I am so happy, so at peace. I'm not afraid anymore because I know Jesus Christ is with me. All the candles we burned and all the prayers we chanted meant nothing. Only God's Son, Jesus, can forgive us or hear us when we pray."

"Where did you learn all this?" Carmen questioned.

"At the mission in the city. First I went to hear the beautiful singing. The words of the songs were satisfying, and I constantly hungered to hear more. The mission workers were always friendly. They simply radiated kindness and were always ready to listen to my problems. But really, Carmen, what made me want what they had, came after something terrible happened." Raquel's voice trembled, and her glowing expression turned thoughtful.

Unknown to the women, someone was listening. Hugo had stationed himself below the kitchen window, anxious to hear everything the women discussed.

"It makes me sad every time I think of Ricardo," Raquel began. "He came from the north, from the old Mayan trading center. Only sixteen years old, he got into wrong company and became involved with a rich Hindu who hires others to smuggle. One time Ricardo kept some of the contraband for himself and was caught. He was beaten severely and left for dead when the mission found him. They took him to their headquarters, nursed him until he was better, then gave him a home with one of the mission families. He learned to know Jesus and became a Christian. He was a likable, hardworking youth, whose love was Jesus Christ. After living at the mission for several months, he wanted to go home and tell his family and friends what God meant to him.

"Ricardo never came back alive. No one knows

what happened. Late one night his body was dumped on the mission steps along with a note saying the same thing would happen to any mission worker who interfered with their men again."

Carmen shuddered as Raquel paused in her story. Smuggling! Her husband was a big-time smuggler!

"What made me see God's love for us is how the mission responded. They prayed. They didn't panic but had prayer meetings for Ricardo's murderers and made plans to contact his family. Sometime later another gang member was seriously hurt and abandoned by his friends. He, too, found his way to the mission. He isn't a Christian yet, but they are caring for him and showing him God's love. Oh, Carmen! God's love and forgiveness is for anyone. He cares about you, about Kevin, about Hugo, and He longs for you to be happy. I do want you to know Jesus Christ's forgiveness!"

Carmen shook her head in agitation, and Raquel grew silent. She sensed Carmen's fear of her husband.

"Is baby Kevin always this good for you?" she asked instead.

Hugo returned to his hammock. *So! Carmen's brother's wife is a Christian like Mister Jay! What does her husband say?* Hugo lay back deep in thought. He had plenty to think about. A lot of questions needed answers, but his head hammered, and it was hard for him to sort through all he had heard. Maybe if he could sleep, his head would clear.

Chapter 13

Stifling midday heat baked the parched jungle, sapping any moisture left after the previous day's searing rays. Muddy water was hauled from the river, boiled, then drunk sparingly. Tempers ran short, alcohol consumption increased, and fights erupted. The longer the rains delayed, the more serious became the villagers' plight. They burned extra candles, entreating God to send rain and appease any sin in the village.

"Mama Donado!" Hugo strode into her kitchen porch, kicking aside a chicken pecking crumbs. "Mama Donado!" He cursed the mess surrounding him and the sodden woman sprawled across the bed.

She won't wake for hours, if at all today, he seethed in disgust. He didn't need her anyway, because he already knew every hiding place in the house. He set to work enlarging the one beneath his old bedroom until he had a six-foot-by-eight-foot hole. He wouldn't ask Mama's permission; he would just bring in his stuff and pay her to keep quiet. "This is safer than at Jay's," he muttered with satisfaction as he replaced the floorboards and pulled the bed back over the hidden, underground storage room before leaving the house.

The drought added greater pressure on Hugo to sell electronics on the black market. Slowly his cash flow increased. Soon Hugo owned both his car and a newer Toyota Landrover.

The money is there if you know how to get it! Hugo congratulated himself.

A second son, Berton, joined the family. He, too, was premature and needed to spend several weeks in the hospital before coming home.

Hugo was proud of his boys and their American names. He showed his pride by treating them well. When Hugo stopped drinking, Carmen changed her mind about leaving. Since Berton's birth, the Millers had returned, and Carmen and Hugo now had their own home. It wasn't as nice as Miss Ida's house, but it was one of the better ones in San Marcos. Since Jay and Ida's return, Carmen spent part of every day with Miss Ida and her daughter, Janice. Hugo wasn't home much, but Carmen didn't mind since she had Miss Ida to talk to. Besides, her older brother Efran, his wife Vilma, and their three children had moved to the village.

"As long as you treat me right and don't drink, I'm willing to stay," Carmen told her husband. Her threat sobered Hugo, filling him with fear at the thought of losing what was dearest to him.

It was late in May before the rains arrived, ending the drought and returning life in San Marcos back to normal. The Ramos River rose, bringing with it San Marcos' floating bridge. Higher and higher the bridge floated until its ends once more rested high up on the river's rocky bank.

"See the cane? Looks good! Right?" Smiling widely the villagers greeted each other with hearty slaps on the back. Ah, it was going to be a good year after all! Their candle-burning had not been in vain. Their prayers had been answered. The steady rains continued to fall each day, turning the fields and jungle a lush green.

Hugo now worked with his uncle and hired one pack boy, Carlos, a fourteen-year-old nephew. Since he no longer needed Barco's boys to pack, the villagers felt cheated and turned against Hugo. Why should he continue using their village when they didn't get a profit? Week after week Hugo passed by their village as he smuggled illegal electronics across from the neighboring country. One night men from Barco felled trees across the road so Hugo couldn't make his usual run. Blind with rage, Hugo gunned his Toyota, smashing into the village party center, sending the thatched roof and supporting posts flying in every direction. The men let Hugo alone after that. They feared the gun he carried and the men he worked with. Neither could they ask the police for help because the villagers themselves were smuggling and wanted no customs agents asking questions. Though they let him alone, their feelings did not change. They hated big-shot Lopez.

When someone moved to the Ameco district who didn't know Lopez, it wasn't long until he was made aware of Lopez's influence. "Lopez? Ya don't know big-shot Lopez? Man! Where ya been? Ya live in the outback? He's short and slim, but has strength to surpass men twice his size. And brains! No one can outsmart Lopez!" The stories grew—some exaggerated, some true, and others completely false.

Lopez was in turn hated, despised, tolerated, and admired, but always considered top man. Most people in the Ameco district only knew *about* Lopez. Only the villagers of Barco, the border patrols, and a few top men in contraband could personally identify him.

One night long after most honest people were asleep, Carlos was alert, waiting. A jaguar's blood-curdling scream far off in the jungle startled him. After hearing the shrill squeal of a terror-stricken peccary, he relaxed, knowing the jaguar was feasting and would hunt no further. Around the bend lay Barco. Carlos was relieved he had met no one since his uncle had dropped him.

"I'll pick you up in two hours," Hugo had promised as he left to meet another contact further upriver. Carlos felt good as he recalled his uncle's parting words. "I know I can count on you." He didn't relish making this contact alone, but he liked that Uncle Hugo treated him like a man. He wouldn't let Hugo down. His uncle had taught him to use his wits, to think ahead, and not to be intimidated. He owed his uncle a lot.

Stealthily he left the Barco road, taking one of the side trails to the river. He didn't want the village dogs barking, announcing his arrival. Carlos grinned as he thought of the repaired party shelter.

Uncle sure let them know they can't mess with us! And they haven't, either. He was proud to be working with someone so important.

"Halt!" The unexpected command rang through the night. Carlos froze in terror as a flashlight beam nearly blinded him. Customs officials! His heart stopped as he caught sight of their badges and two gun barrels pointed right at him.

"Who are you?" barked one official.

Carlos made no answer. Fear paralyzed his tongue.

Roughly he was blindfolded and forced to kneel. As his senses returned he determined nothing would make him talk. Nothing.

"Tell us. Tell us who you are and who you work for."

Carlos didn't move or answer.

"Talk! Talk, or I'll kill you!" Carlos felt cold

metal against his temple and knew this was no idle threat.

I'll die before I tell on Uncle Hugo. I will make Uncle proud, even if I die. Carlos knelt motionless, feigning ignorance of the official's command to talk. A dog barked, and another answered. He caught the rustle of some night animal on the prowl. Then a gun cocked, and he steeled himself for death. Instead, the gun barrel was taken from his head, and he heard retreating footsteps.

The jungle grew silent except for the persistent whine of mosquitoes. Trembling, Carlos reached up to remove his blindfold.

He was alive! Relief washed over him, and he began shaking uncontrollably. His legs gave way, and he crumpled to the ground, crawling into the dense darkness of the jungle. Slowly his heart quit racing. He was alive! The officials hadn't killed him! Strength returned. What should he do next? He must warn Uncle!

I will walk ahead, he planned. *It is not safe for Uncle to come this way. They may be waiting to ambush him.*

The four miles seemed endless. Would he make it? Would he meet the patrols again? He ran until he couldn't run anymore, than he walked until he caught his breath. The turnoff! He had made it! It was only minutes before he recognized the Toyota's whining engine. When Hugo slowed for the turnoff, Carlos jumped up, flagging him down.

"Patrols, Uncle! Patrols!" he blurted as he jumped in and closed the door. Hugo was already turning the Toyota around. Switching off the lights they headed back to the safety of home.

Carlos' account left Hugo shaken. Should he give up smuggling? What if he were ever caught? What else could he do for money?

Chapter 14

Hugo didn't leave the village for several days, feeling safer keeping a low profile. For the first time since Berton was born, he spent an entire day at home. He was appalled at his wife's lack of strength and how often she had to lie down and rest. For the first time he became aware of the deep shadows around her eyes and the way her skin stretched tautly across her cheekbones.

"Carmen, I am taking you to the city to find a doctor," his statement surprised her. "You are not well. We must get help. I don't want to lose you."

Tears filled Carmen's eyes. She was not used to a husband's kindness and his concern overwhelmed her.

"We need to find a doctor for Carmen," Hugo told Jay. "I did not know she was sick. I've been too busy," he added lamely.

Jay looked at his wife silently, begging her to say what he could not. Ida smiled before turning to Hugo. "I'm glad you are taking your wife to a doctor," she chose her words carefully. She did not want to make him feel she was blaming him. "Since Berton's birth she hasn't regained her strength. Hugo, your wife is a dear friend. I've been worried! She, well, she has been losing strength," Ida's gentle words held no reproach, only loving concern.

"Why hasn't Carmen said anything?" Hugo asked in frustration.

"She didn't want to worry or upset you. You have been busy." Her quiet rebuke took the sting away. "Do you have a doctor?" Ida questioned.

"No," Hugo replied. "Do you?" Maybe Mister Jay would help! Hope surged through him.

"I'm sorry, we don't, unless you would want to take her to the doctor I went to for malaria. Maybe that would be best." Ida brightened. "If she needs a specialist, he would refer her to one."

"Let us know how we can help," Jay offered as Hugo took the doctor's phone number. "Ida and I will be glad to go with you. And we are praying for Carmen, Hugo. God loves you both and knows all about her sickness. He cares about each one in your family."

"Thank you," Hugo mumbled, self-conscious at their kindness. That evening Hugo attended Jay's church service. Jay did not see Hugo among the circle of faces; nevertheless, from outside Hugo heard every word. It shocked him to find Efran and Vilma inside the chapel. How long had they been attending? Did Carmen know? Why didn't she tell him? Why didn't she tell him anything? He was her husband! Maybe after she felt better, she would talk. It never dawned on Hugo that he could be responsible for Carmen's timidity. Even before their marriage, all his time was consumed with work. Hugo was used to giving orders and being obeyed. He was not used to giving of himself.

Almost as soon as they had been married, a wall had begun between him and his wife. She never knew what her husband was doing, where he was, or when he would be home. Carmen had learned early that Hugo expected her at home whenever he appeared at the door hungry. He expected a hot meal immediately; that much she knew. But she knew little else of her sons' father. Hugo provided for the physical well-being of his family. He was proud of his sons and wife, but never understood the need to provide for their emotional well-being. They were a family in name only.

Restlessly, Hugo listened to Jay explain the parable of the lost sheep. He had read the same story in Jay's Bible.

"The lost sheep was precious to his shepherd," Jay said earnestly. "The shepherd sought it until he found it and brought it back with joy. In Jesus' time, the sheep were the shepherd's responsibility, and he was required to bring home the fleece if one died. No sacrifice was too great to recover the lost sheep.

"We are even more precious to Jesus. Knowing we are hopelessly lost in sin, He pursues us, longing to restore us to the safety of His fold. When one sinner is found, He brings him back with great rejoicing. All heaven rejoices, showing us the great love Jesus has for every person."

Jay's explanation was new to Hugo. He would have to think it through. *Is it true what Mister Jay said? Does God really care about me and about Carmen's sickness? How would He know about it all? Why would God care about anything so small?* It was perplexing.

Maybe tomorrow he would find some answers. Tomorrow, Jays planned to go to the city with them. But the next day brought heaviness.

"Mama!" Kevin sobbed when he heard Carmen had to stay behind at the hospital. "Mama, Mama!"

Hugo was not used to caring for the boys. His arms were already full with Berton, and he felt helpless as his older son clung to Carmen's bed, unwilling to move.

"Don't worry about the boys," he heard Ida say to his wife. "Jay and I will be home to help whenever Hugo needs someone." Her words lifted the heaviness enveloping him. Even Kevin quieted and took Janice's hand as they left the hospital.

It had been an exhausting day for the children. Carmen had been referred immediately to a specialist. Numerous tests were done, and the waiting had seemed endless. All three children were sound asleep before they left the city. Kevin and Janice curled up on blankets in the back of the car, their hands still tightly clasped together.

Even the adults were silent. Neither of the Millers wished to infringe on Hugo's privacy. The test results wouldn't be back for several weeks, but they all felt Carmen's illness was far more serious than they had thought. Ida closed her eyes and in the silence talked with her heavenly Father, pleading for Hugo and Carmen's spiritual and physical needs. "Use us, Lord," she prayed. "and give us wisdom to handle each situation to Thy honor and glory."

"Can the boys stay here while I talk to Mama Donado and Efran?" Hugo asked when they had finished eating supper.

"Certainly!" Ida responded. "And, Hugo, if you need anything, don't be afraid to ask. If you need meals or a place for the boys, we are here."

"Thank you, Miss Ida. You have already helped very much."

Hugo left the missionary's house, tempted to let the boys live there. Never would he let Mama keep the boys. She couldn't be trusted to stay sober. Maybe Vilma would keep them for the next few days until he could make other arrangements. Before leaving Efrans', it was decided Hugo would take the boys at night and Vilma during the day.

Hugo had never taken complete responsibility for his sons, but he learned quickly. He threw himself wholeheartedly into his new role as father and brought security to his small sons. Kevin went with his daddy everywhere he possibly could. He sobbed for his daddy, clinging to him when they needed to be separated. Hugo was experiencing a love for his children he never dreamed was possible. All his loneliness as a child came back to him. Now that he was needed at home, he worked only during the day, determining anew never to drink again. Each night he slept between his sons, both cuddled close to him. He reveled in their closeness, their dependence upon him, and their delight with having their father near.

Several times Hugo traveled to the city to visit Carmen. The new tenderness he felt towards his sons carried over to his wife. Despite her weakness Carmen began to feel better. The husband and wife began to talk to each other. Healing came to Carmen's heart as the wall between them crumbled. Now she longed to get well and come home.

When the test results came in, the doctor broke the news gently. "I'm sorry. Your wife has colon cancer. After surgery we will need to start treatments."

Cancer! Fear gripped Carmen.

"Cancer!" Suffocating anger welled up in Hugo,

filling him with a blinding rage at God. Was God going to take his sons' mother? Was this Jay's God who loved them and cared about them? It wouldn't happen! He would use all his savings. He would get the best doctors to care for his wife. He would do whatever he could. He didn't need Jay's God if this was how He treated people.

Chapter 15

"Mister Hugo!" Five-year-old Janice called from the stair steps from where she was playing with her doll family. Hugo stopped, waiting to hear what she had to tell him. He chuckled as he regarded her dancing blue eyes. Her freckled face had a wide smile, revealing the gaping hole where she had just lost a tooth.

"Aunt Minnie is coming on the airplane!" Janice's words tumbled over each other in her excitement. "And Mister Hugo, real soon I get either a baby brother like Berton or a baby sister!" There, all her news was spilled out and she beamed at him with shining eyes, trusting him to share in her pleasure.

Hugo patted her golden head. "Pretty big news for such a small girl."

Janice's laughter bubbled over. "Mama says I'm getting big, not small!"

"So you are, so you are," Hugo agreed. He hurried on, not wanting Miss Ida to come out and ask about Carmen. He didn't want to talk, he was still too angry at God.

Carmen came home from the hospital, weak from her first round of treatments. Hugo paid one of the village women to cook and look after the boys. The surgery, the six-week hospital stay, the hired help, and now the treatments were fast draining the fifteen thousand dollars in his savings.

He needed to make big money fast. He knew where such a job was waiting but had never wanted to get involved before. Now he felt he had no choice. That week he attended one of Pedro's parties, found his job, was given a permit, and consented to return the next day.

"I need to be gone tomorrow," he told his wife when he returned. "Maybe it will take one day, maybe two, I don't know. But don't worry. I will come as soon as I finish." The next morning he rose before dawn. Going into his sons' room, he gazed at the sleeping boys. He touched first one tousled head and then the other. His hand trembled. If he were caught, his sons would have no father. Should he give it up? He retraced his steps, reluctant to leave Carmen. He paused at the bedroom door to watch his sleeping wife. He was proud of his family. He didn't want to go, but knew of no other way to get the money they needed. Finally he tore himself away. He was doing this job for Carmen. With a heavy heart he left the house.

Hugo had never welded, but it didn't take long

for him to learn how to spot-weld containers of drugs into the bottom of the four propane tanks his permit allowed him to take over legally. The welding didn't take long, neither did the refilling of the tanks or loading them onto the waiting dory. The delay lay in knowing when it was safe to cross without running into border patrols. His contact man would be waiting across the river. Only after he delivered his tanks would he be paid and free to go. Hugo sweated through the morning, trying to decide when to leave. Patrols were everywhere. He made himself useful, blending in with the workers, acting as if his job was solely on the wharf, loading and unloading. Should he go or stay? Should he wait until late tonight or early morning? His mind kept returning to Carmen and the boys. He couldn't shake the uneasy feeling that plagued him. He knew he was doing wrong. Snatches of a song he had heard at the chapel tormented him.

There's a God who's standing at heaven's door . . .
He sees each mortal with a searching eye,
You can't do wrong and get by.
. . . Nothing hidden can be,
Everything He doth see . . .

Can't I do anything without thinking of Jay's God? he asked himself in disgust.

After these tanks are delivered, it will be the first and last drug smuggling I do, he vowed as he waited for a safe time to cross.

A sudden storm brought heavy, gray clouds boiling overhead and an unexpected downpour. The rain fell in torrents, sending workers on the run for cover. Now! The time was right. Swiftly Hugo untied his dory and swung it downstream. Sheets of rain wiped out all sight of the shore, giving him the needed cover to leave unnoticed. By the time the rain let up, Hugo had rowed far enough down the winding river that he could no longer be seen from the legal crossing. He stopped paddling only long enough to dip out most of the water sloshing in the dory bottom before he pushed on. Fifteen minutes later he pulled his dory into the hidden cove of overhanging palms. He had made it!

Transferring the goods and payment took only minutes, and Hugo headed home. He was alive and had eight hundred dollars safely in his pocket. Yet there was an inner heaviness he couldn't shake off.

"Never again," he vowed. He was exhausted and felt like an old man. He hated the feeling. Was he weakening or getting sick?

Several busy weeks had elapsed since little Janice had stopped Hugo to share her good news. Hugo was rarely home during the day and purposely kept himself too busy to visit with the Millers. If there was a God who cared about his family, he didn't want any of His care, Hugo reasoned. Carmen's illness and God's care did not add up. Since God wasn't answering the Millers' prayers, he wanted no part of God.

The village grew quiet as darkness settled over San Marcos. The moon rose and one by one families extinguished their lights, seeking rest. Carmen and the boys were fast asleep, but Hugo's restlessness drove sleep far away. As he heated some coffee, he wished instead for a beer. He knew there was none in the house. Maybe he should see if Mama Donado was awake. She would have one. One wouldn't hurt him. Maybe it would settle his nerves so he could sleep.

Loud knocking on their door startled him. Police? Panic swept through him before he recognized Jay's voice.

"It's Jay. Hugo, are you still up?"

Quickly Hugo unlocked the door, sensing trouble. Jays never came over at this late hour. "I saw your light was still on," Jay said, his voice strained. "I just came from the hospital. Our baby lived only two hours. I need to return, and I need gas. Can I get some from you? I would have waited until morning to come but wanted to tell Minnie and Janice about the baby. By the time I left the city, all the gas pumps were closed."

"Is your wife okay?" Hugo asked in disbelief.

"Yes, Ida's fine and we praise God for it. We would have wished for our little son to be healthy. Our hearts are sad because we longed to bring him home and care for him. We will miss him dearly. But Hugo, we know our baby son is in heaven where he will be safe forever. That knowledge makes it easier to accept his passing. Someday we will see him again." Though Jay's heart ached with grief, and his voice grew husky with emotion, the calm radiance on his face astonished Hugo. It was beyond understanding.

"I'm sorry about your baby," Hugo answered awkwardly. "Come, I'll get you some gas."

The death of the Millers' baby softened the villagers toward their American neighbors. Most of the village women had also buried babies and grieved for them. The quiet burial, the joy radiating from the parents' tearstained faces as they sang beside the tiny coffin, and their continued devotion to God left a deep impression.

Efran and Vilma were deeply touched. They were ready to step out for God and be part of Jay and Ida Miller's church. Both wanted to surrender their hearts and lives to the One who died for man's sin. Both asked the Lord Jesus to cleanse their sinful hearts and make them new creatures. They rejoiced to claim God's promise, "If thou shalt confess with thy mouth the Lord Jesus, and shalt believe in thine heart that God hath raised him from the dead, thou shalt be saved."

Vilma was the first village woman to follow Ida's example of wearing the prayer veiling, the outward sign of her commitment to fulfill God's command of submission as taught in

1 Corinthians 11.

"Why do you wear that white veil? I thought it was just the American gringo's way!" As village women bombarded Vilma with questions, she explained the teaching in God's Word.

Efran and Vilma's home became a happy oasis as they lived for God and taught their children from the Bible. Their lives drew other villagers to come to the services held in the thatch-roofed church house.

Hugo found his anger abating. He watched his brother-in-law's family closely and couldn't deny there was a change in Efran and Vilma's lives. Kindness was visibly displayed. Efran no longer lounged around the tienda with other men. His temper seemed to have disappeared, and he was always ready to lend a helping hand.

When Hugo heard that his brother-in-law apologized to neighbor Alexandro, he was finally convinced Efran's belief in Jesus Christ was real. Shortly after buying land and moving to San Marcos, Efran had become so furious with his neighbor that the villagers were afraid someone would get killed. Alexandro had claimed some of Efran's land and planted it in cane along with his own. The feud had never been settled. Since then, both men had despised each other.

Hugo chuckled as he recalled Alexandro shaking his head and sputtering, "Those gringos must be making Efran loco! He gave me his land! I can't believe it! I can't believe it! He must be going loco." Efran's peace-loving offer loosened Alexandro's tongue to unknowingly acknowledge what he had earlier so hotly denied.

It also brought Hugo under greater conviction. For a long time he had been reading the Bible, studying what he heard, looking for answers, and watching the Millers. He knew truth was taught at the little chapel. He also believed it was the right way to live, but the need for money held him back from openly attending services or committing himself.

Chapter 16

Carmen needed more expensive treatments. Hugo couldn't make enough money selling electronics and flour to cover the high bills. Drug-dealing offered the best means for big cash, but Hugo was reluctant. Drug-smuggling was dangerous. In addition, he knew it was wrong. But he considered smuggling food or electronics as altogether different from smuggling drugs. Yet he didn't know where else to turn for help. During this indecision he bumped into his old Hindu friend, Zang.

"Our people need someone to help with the dead," Zang offered when he heard about Hugo's money needs. The Hindus burn the bodies of their dead. "Your job would be to bring firewood, get everything ready, then stay until the body is cremated. We pay well," Zang continued. "Still, no one wants to do it. Everyone's afraid of the spirits of the dead."

Five times, Hugo was called on to prepare the final exodus for a departed Hindu. Each time it took all day to haul the necessary firewood. The ritual demanded a carefully laid pyre of wood, each layer at cross angles to the one below until it stood almost as high as a man. On top was placed the empty casket, filled with more wood. The body lay in the open on top of it all. When the fire was lit, the departed one's family, friends, and relatives marched around and around the roaring fire chanting in their native tongue.

Hindu body-burning took place after dark, making it an even more grotesque sight. The carefully stacked, dry firewood became a chimney, drawing the fire upward in its roaring blaze. Fire engulfed the body as the flames leapt skyward into the darkness. Hugo stayed for hours watching the fire until nothing was left but a mound of ashes. He never asked any questions about this custom. It was their practice. As long as they paid him five hundred dollars for each body burned, he didn't care what they did with their dead. He needed the money for Carmen, and that was all that counted.

Hugo returned to smuggling at night again because there was less chance of being detected. Darkness became his friend and protector. He enjoyed the challenge, relentlessly pursuing bigger and better contacts. Carlos continued working for him. Several times Carlos' father, Ian, went with them to help pack out an extra large delivery of electronics. Zang bought all Hugo's merchandise. His own network was so large that there was always a demand for more.

One stormy August night Hugo returned late to the sleeping village. At the top of the hill, entering San Marcos, he cut the Landrover's engine, coasting downhill around the corner and into his driveway. Entering stealthily was routine, another precaution Hugo took when the hour was late. Tonight he didn't bother unloading the jeep. He would be delivering the goods tomorrow.

In the night, there was suddenly a loud hammering and shouting. "Open! Customs Defense Force." The pounding on the door finally penetrated Hugo's deep sleep. Instantly he leaped from bed, following an escape plan he had mentally prepared for himself. He crept through the boys' bedroom. Unlocking the window, he climbed through and noiselessly lowered himself to the ground. A hedge of bougainvillea hugged the boys' bedroom wall, giving him enough protection to slip through and run for Carlos' house.

"Wake up! Customs! Police!" Hugo hissed through the flimsy partition of Carlos' sleeping room. Ian, too, was instantly aroused and grabbed his gun. The three returned to Hugo's house where the waiting officials were still pounding on the door.

"I'll grab the man at the side," Ian whispered. "Make a lot of noise, you two. Scare them off," he ordered.

Swiftly he made his move. Before the officer

knew what was happening, Ian clamped his burly hand across his mouth, threw his gun to Hugo, and dragged his prisoner around the corner of the darkened house.

"Over here! Over here!" Carlos screamed again and again.

Hugo fired the gun into the air—once, twice, and three times. "I'm here!" he returned the scream.

"I have you covered," Ian bellowed from the corner where he held his prisoner.

Chaos reigned as Carlos and Hugo ran around the neighboring houses shouting, "Come on! We have you surrounded. We have you surrounded!" The gun shots convinced the remaining officer they were indeed surrounded. Better to surrender now and leave with their lives. They could always return later with military help.

Boldly Hugo confronted the Defense Police with a bright beam from his flashlight. The officer dropped his gun and raised his arms in surrender. Targeting the officer with his gun, he pointed the way back to their vehicle.

"Follow!" Ian barked as he released his prisoner.

"I'm starting this car," Hugo's cold, commanding voice left no room for doubt. "You leave. We will follow you. Don't return, or we'll shoot to kill."

"Stay here, son," Ian instructed Carlos. Jumping into Hugo's Landrover, they followed the departing customs vehicles.

When Carlos entered Hugo's house, he found Carmen and the boys weeping hysterically. "Hugo's fine, I promise," he comforted them. Then he told Carmen what had happened. "We scared them!" he boasted. "Uncle, Dad, and I sure scared them!"

Carlos took the boys back to bed, promising them he would stay until morning.

After Hugo and Ian had made sure the Customs Defense Force vehicle was well on its way to Ameco, they returned to Barco, taking with them the electronics they had just brought across the border.

"Don't return," Pedro warned. "They'll bring in the military. You are now a hunted man."

Ian blanched, not fully recognizing the seriousness of their situation until now. "I'm not going back," he determined. "They are not looking for me, but I'm going to play it safe. I have a cousin living in the city. Carlos can do what he wants. It's just him and me anyway."

Hugo shrugged. Ian could do as he pleased, but he had a family. Was Pedro right? Was he a hunted man?

Restlessly he waited for word from San Marcos. Poor Carmen, she was so fearful! He berated himself for being in trouble. Where had he slipped? Who had squealed on him?

It was two o'clock the following morning before

Carlos came. "It's bad, Uncle," he greeted him gravely. "Early yesterday morning soldiers swarmed our village. They took your Toyota at home and they also got your jeep at Barco. They questioned everyone, but no one knows where Lopez lives or what happened last night. The villagers said they were sleeping, that it must have been men from a neighboring village making trouble." Carlos laughed as he recalled the frightened officers surrendering to two men and himself. But he quickly sobered as he continued.

"They questioned Mama Donado. She was sober enough to know what they wanted but drunk enough not to be afraid. She got mad when they wanted to search her house. Did she ever scream at them! She said she was getting the police from the capital if they ever came back again and accused her. She was innocent, and doesn't even know who Lopez is! She told them they were looking in the wrong village. They seem to know a lot about you, Uncle, especially if they went to Mama Donado's."

Hugo remained silent, deep in thought. For the first time, he was truly afraid. There was nothing he could do, and he had nowhere to go. God's Word spoke pleadingly to Hugo's stubborn heart. *God is my refuge and strength, a very present help in time of trouble. The heart is deceitful . . . and desperately wicked, who can know it?*

For the first time, he wished he could change

places with his brother-in-law, Efran. He wished he had quit smuggling. He wished all he did was grow cane. He knew his life was black with sin. His wickedness tormented him. He was sure God wanted nothing to do with him. He was Hugo Donado, known as Lopez, the biggest smuggler in Ameco district. But today he was nothing, a hunted man without home, friends, or money. He couldn't trust anyone.

"Tell Carmen I'll come back when it's safe. Stay with them since your dad went to the city. I have money hidden beneath the boys' bedroom floor. Move the rug and feel for a loose board. Be careful, Carlos. Stay around the village because someone might be watching you. And tell Mister Jay to keep an eye on Carmen. If she needs anything, she can tell them. Tell him I have to be gone for awhile. I'll come home when I can. I'll tap four times on the boys' window. When you hear me, open the window, and I'll come in that way."

Carlos left as soon as Hugo finished giving him instructions. He wanted to be home safe in bed before daylight. Slippery mud covered the jungle trail. Night sounds and looming dark shapes terrified him. Was that an officer or soldier hiding? Were those footsteps he heard? Surely he could hear someone breathing! Stealthily he crept homeward. It took him two hours to make the usual half-hour trek, for at every noise he stopped, making sure it was safe before moving on. If he didn't hurry, dawn would be breaking before he arrived.

A rooster crowed as he staggered through the hedge and hoisted himself through the window.

I made it! was his last thought before sleep claimed his exhausted body.

Chapter 17

Two weeks after chasing the Customs Defense authorities from his doorstep, Hugo returned to San Marcos. He had to see his family again. Slipping into the village under cover of darkness, he stayed for several hours.

"I am better, Hugo." Carmen clung to him, reassuring her husband that she no longer needed further treatments. She felt the lines etched on his face. It was too dark to see, but somehow she knew he felt beaten. It worried her. "When can you come home? The boys beg for you every day," she pleaded. "Besides, I think they are mixed up. Miss Ida says the military is looking for Lopez."

"Carmen," Hugo slowly answered his wife, "I . . . am . . . Lopez."

She gasped, her eyes widening in fright. "Why? I don't understand!"

"I am Lopez. Big shot. Top contraband man in Ameco district." He spat out the bitter words. "What did it get me? Can't take care of my family, can't see my boys, or come home. I'm like a peccary, hunted and on the run. I changed my name, Carmen, as a precaution. I'm sorry that I got us into this mess." Hugo's whispered words touched her. She sensed his shame and helplessness. Gently she reached for his hand.

"Mister Jay can help, can't he?"

Hugo didn't answer. Finally he rose. "I want to see the boys," he said. Together they went to the boys' room. Softly Hugo touched first Kevin, than Berton. Berton whimpered, moving closer to his brother before settling back to sleep. Faint moonlight spilled across the children, revealing their sweet innocence. A stab of pain shot through Hugo. What would become of his boys? Would they need to suffer because of him?

"I need to leave," Hugo said wearily. "I need to find a safe place. I need to find work. And, Carmen," he continued in agitation, "attend church with Efrans. Take the boys. Learn all you can." So intense were his feelings that he forgot he was talking to his wife. Instead of showing loving concern for his family he sounded like a commander, harsh and demanding. Resentment replaced Carmen's sympathy. Why should she do what her husband wouldn't? She forgot her suggestion of asking for Mister Jay's help. If he was going to start ordering her around again, he may as well leave!

When Hugo left before dawn, there was tension between them. Hugo was unwilling to confide in

Carmen. He carried a burden threatening to engulf him. Yet as he helplessly floundered and classed himself a complete failure, he defended himself instead of consoling his wife.

Not grasping the seriousness of Hugo's smuggling activity, Carmen blamed him for leaving her alone with the boys. She deliberately stayed away from Efrans and Jays. No one was going to tell her what to do. The thought of taking the boys and leaving returned to tempt her.

Three months passed. Hiding, moving from place to place, and living in fear had aged Hugo until he lost his youthful appearance. It wasn't safe to return home, and he hadn't heard a word from his family. He ached to see his children. Finally the longing grew so great that he again made plans to return.

Carmen had also changed. Living alone had lost its attraction, and she again sought out Miss Ida's companionship, even taking the boys to Millers' church on Sundays. Vilma proved to be a real sister, sharing many hours with her and the boys.

Hugo's absence was not considered unusual by other villagers. Village men often left to find work at the coast or along the *cayes* (barrier reefs) where the waters teamed with fish. And they saw nothing abnormal for Carmen to be left alone to care for her boys. Hugo's mother lived alone next door, and many other women in the village shared the same lot.

Any rumors that Hugo was wanted in connection with Lopez were dismissed. Lopez was one of the rich. Hugo's Landrover proved he was better off than most of the villagers, but none were aware of his involvement in anything other than buying cheap flour and corn. He was smart, they acknowledged. If he smuggled, so did many others. It was a way of life. Things were cheaper from the neighboring country, and everyone was glad to buy the least expensive goods.

Hugo had no known enemies in the village of San Marcos. His enemies came from Barco and farther away. In transporting electronics he drove hard bargains. Smaller buyers were pushed back as he took the highest resale goods. Many times they were outwitted by his shrewd dealing. Lopez was a big shot, but hated by several who longed to destroy him.

One such person was Zang. He had become jealous of Hugo's growing power among the top circle. Unknown to Hugo, someone was watching as he slipped into San Marcos. Even before he reached his house, a man was speeding to Ameco to inform the police of Lopez's whereabouts.

Hugo slipped through the hedge and tapped on the bedroom window. No one answered. The window slid up at his touch, and he crawled inside. Standing by his sons' bedside, he thought of the times he had shared their bed when

Carmen was in the hospital. Kevin would soon be four. Hugo's heart ached with loneliness. He noted Carlos's absence. Did he no longer live in the village? Hugo longed to hold his boys, to tussle with them, to feel their little arms tight around his neck. Quietly he crawled into bed between them. It was so good to be close to them. Both boys snuggled up against him, and before long Hugo joined them in sleep.

Several hours later Hugo awoke to knocking. Startled, he lay in bed listening as Carmen answered the door.

"We have a search warrant for Lopez." The words chilled him.

"I told you he doesn't live here!" Carmen answered in exasperation. "Only I and the boys live here."

"We still have to search," the police apologized.

Hugo listened numbly as they entered. *If I move, the boys will waken. Can I play dumb and keep sleeping?* He drew his legs up beside Kevin's, burrowing his head down under the blankets until only his nose and forehead were free. Feigning deep sleep, he made himself as small as possible.

Footsteps sounded. A beam of flashlight played across the bed. Holding his breath, he lay motionless, willing himself to relax. "Just boys," the whispers of the officers reached him. Footsteps retreated. Hugo pinched himself to make sure he wasn't dreaming. For the first time, he was thank-

115

ful for his small size.

"Why do you keep coming back?" Carmen's question to the officers startled Hugo. So there had been earlier searches! This wasn't the first!

"Lady, we were informed he came here tonight. Sorry. We won't bother you again. This is the last time we are coming back! Someone is tricking us!" The disgruntled officers left, upset at looking like fools.

He heard the soft pad of Carmen's footsteps coming towards the bedroom to check on the boys.

"Carmen, don't be scared. It's me, Hugo." He whispered softly from the bed. He heard Carmen's sharp intake of breath as she stopped. "I'm in bed with the boys," he continued gently. "Wait where you are until I get up, so I don't wake them."

Hugo didn't want his wife to scream with fright. She dare not make any commotion. Quietly he continued talking. "I'm home, Carmen. I came several hours ago but didn't want to disturb you, so I crawled into bed with the boys." He had now reached his wife and gently put his arms around her. "I'm home, Carmen. It's me," he whispered soothingly against her hair. "You don't have to be afraid."

As he led Carmen from the boys' room, he could feel her trembling. Fearing the shock was too much for her, Hugh picked her up and carried her to their room.

"I'm home to stay, Carmen. I'm not leaving

again," he continued, waiting till she stopped shaking. Slowly she grew calm. "I've lived a wicked life, Carmen. I haven't treated you right, but I love you. I love the boys, and I'm going to stay home now. We are going to go to church with Efrans and Jays."

"Will the . . . police . . . take . . . you?" Carmen stammered in terror at the thought of Hugo being thrown into jail.

"I don't know, Carmen. But remember the words from the Bible on Mister Jay's wall, 'I will trust, and not be afraid.' I want to trust in Jay's God. If it's possible, I want to trust. He must be watching over us. The officers thought I was one of the boys. If God wasn't on our side tonight . . ." his voice grew silent. "At least someone was," he finished.

Chapter 18

"**H**ugo!" Jay greeted his neighbor. "It's mighty good to see you again. We've all missed you." He hoped he wasn't showing too much surprise at seeing Hugo.

He was saddened at the pronounced change in his neighbor. If he hadn't met him face to face, he would easily have passed him by without recognition. His shoulder-length hair hadn't changed, but he now sported a mustache, and an untrimmed shock of hair fell over his forehead, ending just at his eyebrows. His wild appearance made Jay's heart cry in sorrow, "Lord, bring conviction to this young man. He is dear to me. He has great potential. Oh, Lord, where have I failed in reaching him? Show me, use me." Under Jay's compassionate gaze, Hugo lowered his eyes, unable to face his neighbor. He felt wicked.

Daylight has a way of dispelling the fears of darkness. In the following days Hugo found himself forgetting his promises to Carmen. Hadn't he heard the police say they weren't coming back? As weeks passed without disturbance, he forgot his months of living on the run. The village seemed safe. Hugo entered the flow of life in San Marcos—helping Efran cut cane, fishing from the Ramos, and lounging away the evenings at the tienda. He did hold fast to two of his resolutions: not drinking and not smuggling.

His mama's ever-present bottle and surly, obnoxious behavior filled Hugo with renewed determination never to touch the vile stuff again. His abstinence also made him feel good. He was strong enough to resist this temptation. Why attend Jay's church? He could overcome his wicked ways himself. After all, he had taken care of himself and Carmen thus far. Even the doctor pronounced Carmen cured. Why change?

Carmen's happiness at having her husband home again dimmed as he once again became the demanding, domineering husband she had formerly feared.

"Where's dinner?" Hugo yelled, late one morning when Carmen returned from visiting Miss Ida.

"Dinner!" Carmen sputtered. "It's only 11 o'clock!"

"I want it now! You are my wife! When I come home to eat, you are to be here! Don't forget!" Hugo spat out the angry words. Stalking out the door, he slammed it shut, cursing his wife. He wanted to go into Ameco with the cane trucks. Well, he would just go!

Kevin and Berton clung to Carmen in terror. They didn't understand why Daddy acted like this. Why did he scream and scare them? Their young minds were confused. Why couldn't Daddy always be nice like Janice's daddy? Or like Uncle Efran?

Carmen was angry. Hugo had promised to go with Jays to church. He had said he loved her. He had said he was wicked and wanted to trust Jay's God. He didn't keep his word, and she was fed up. Angrily she fixed dinner and waited for Hugo, but she waited in vain.

I'm leaving, she decided. *I'm not staying with such a husband.*

"Come, boys, eat your rice. How would you like to go to Grandma's in Caro?"

"Yes!" the boys cried in unison, clapping their hands. By the time the boys had eaten, Carmen was packed, ready to leave. She didn't even clean up the kitchen. "Let Hugo," she fumed. "He was the one who had wanted an early dinner anyway."

"Stay here, boys. I will be right back," she promised as she hurried to Elena's house. Elena was the only woman she knew with spending money. Hopefully she would let her borrow enough for bus fare to Caro.

"You'll probably need twenty dollars," Elena said as she gave her the money. She gloated at the thought of Carmen and Hugo having trouble. Why else wouldn't Carmen have enough money?

Maybe Carmen would leave for good. She hoped so. Maybe she would still have a chance with Hugo.

It was evening when Hugo caught a ride to San Marcos. Before he entered the dark house, he knew something was wrong. Carmen was always home in the evenings! He looked in dismay at the messy kitchen where dirty dishes and cold food sat on the table. *So, Carmen did make dinner,* he thought remorsefully, recalling his angry words.

The boys' bureau drawers were hanging open, and, yes, clothing was missing! Frantically he checked Carmen's clothes. They, too, were gone. Hugo groaned. *Where has she gone? If only I hadn't lost my temper! I must find her!*

"Were Carmen and the boys here this afternoon?" Hugo questioned Miss Ida.

"No, she wasn't. She was here in the morning," Ida answered. "Is something wrong?" she asked, noting the misery in her neighbor's face.

"She's gone," Hugo replied. "It's my fault. I got mad at her, and now she's gone." For the first time, he was willing to acknowledge responsibility for his actions.

"Hugo, both you and Carmen need someone bigger than yourselves to guide you. You both need Jesus Christ. I'm saying this because Jay and I love you. We want you and Carmen and your boys to have a happy home. We want you and Carmen to experience the happiness that comes only when you personally know Jesus." Ida's pleading words struck deep within Hugo's unhappy soul. He could read genuine concern in Miss Ida. For a fleeting moment he was ready to surrender.

But what would people think of you, Hugo? Though you were once the scorned village shrimp, now you are admired, another voice within reminded him.

"We are having church services at the Blanco village," Hugo heard Ida saying. "They start tomorrow, Hugo. Won't you come along?"

"I must find Carmen," Hugo shrugged. "We'll see."

At the tienda, Elena accosted Hugo. "How long are Carmen and the boys planning to be gone?" she asked coyly.

Hugo scowled. What did Elena know of Carmen? She interpreted his frown to mean displeasure towards Carmen and babbled on, "If I were a man, and my wife ran off on me, I'd sure let her go."

Hugo's face darkened. What was this woman saying? Elena's courage increased. She had Hugo on her side!

"A woman that runs away isn't worth anything. She shames her man. I would just let her live at Mama's! There are other women who would gladly cook for . . ."

Hugo spun around, thoroughly repulsed at her

brazenness. He now knew where Carmen was.

The four-hour bus ride to Caro gave Hugo time to think. Conflict raged in his heart. Part of him wanted to heed Miss Ida's advice. He longed for happiness between him and Carmen, but another part held back. He had worked so hard at establishing himself. Why should he throw it all away?

But am I really anything? he wondered. *The officers are on the lookout for me. I can't return to my circle of friends. I am hated in Barco. Someone's been following me, or how else did they know the night I returned home? Will I ever be safe?*

Hugo weighed each side. Whenever he determined not to give in to Miss Ida, he would remember some Bible verses he had studied from Jay's Bible.

"I'll go to Blanco," he resolved as the bus stopped at Caro. "If Carmen will come home, I promise to attend those meetings with Jay."

Carmen did return. Not because she wanted to, but because her mama wasn't at all happy with her leaving Hugo. "You belong in San Marcos," she scolded. "If Papa learns why you are here, he'll send you right back. Every man beats his wife; that's how life is," was all the sympathy Carmen received.

Chapter 19

"Tomorrow, we'll go tomorrow," Hugo promised Jay when he offered them a ride to the meetings. "Carmen and the boys are still tired from the bus ride," he explained, knowing it was only an excuse.

That night at the meetings Jay shared his burden for the Hugo Donado family. The Christians prayed together, interceding for the souls of this struggling family. While they were in earnest prayer, Hugo was making promises too.

"Sure, I can work for you this week," he said gladly. His Uncle Ian had invited him to the city to learn woodworking. Elated, he hung up the phone, completely forgetting his promise to Jay. His uncle wanted him to learn woodworking! Another challenge! He already looked forward to it.

Tuesday afternoon Jay knocked again at his neighbors' door.

"I'm sorry, my uncle needs me to work in the city," Hugo explained. "I'm going tomorrow, so we can't come."

"We will be home by nine o'clock," Jay kindly explained. "It won't be late."

"I need to get up early to catch a ride into Ameco," Hugo answered quickly.

"I'll take you in," Jay offered. "The city bus doesn't leave until ten o'clock. Think about it; we'll stop again before we leave."

The Millers did not eat supper that evening. Instead they spent the time in prayer.

When it was time to leave, Jay walked over to the Donados again. Carmen answered the door but looked nervously to her husband for an answer.

"We're not ready," Hugo apologized.

"I'm early," Jay smiled warmly. "If I bring the Blazer over in ten minutes, is that enough time?" Grudgingly, Hugo nodded consent.

It took a half hour to make the trip to the little village of Blanco, tucked securely into the jungle on the east side of Ameco. The last mile and a half found them bouncing over rutted roads. Hugo shifted nervously on the seat, berating himself for coming. He had never entered Jay's church—only listened from the outside. Apprehension filled him until he broke out in a cold sweat.

"Welcome, friend. I am Brother Esteban. Welcome to our service." The small Spanish man standing by the doorway of Blanco's chapel reached out a hand to each person entering.

Hugo felt the warmth in his handshake and

smile. His nervousness receded as he found himself curious to learn more of this compelling man who reminded him of himself. He was even more astonished to learn he was the preacher. Hugo had expected another gringo like Jay to speak, but on finding a Spanish man he sat up straighter, not wanting to miss a word he said.

Quietness reigned in the Blazer as they headed home. Jay and Ida did not want to infringe on their neighbors' privacy. Instead, they prayed that the spiritual insight Brother Esteban had presented to the congregation was taking root in the Donados' hearts.

Suddenly, bright lights flashed from the roadside ahead. Jay hit the brakes, stopping inches from an armed policeman waving his machine gun. It was a police check.

"Where did you come from? Where are you going?" the policeman barked. Several other officers with guns surrounded the Blazer.

"We were attending Bible preaching at Blanco," Jay calmly answered. "We are returning home to San Marcos." The officer shone his light across the passengers.

"Show your papers."

Without hesitation Jay handed over the mission vehicle registration and his passport. After careful inspection the officer returned the papers and lowered his gun, waving them on.

"Now what?" Ida broke the silence.

"Don't know," Jay answered. "Must be looking for someone."

"Did they stop you last night?" Hugo spoke up, uneasy at being caught in the road check.

"No," Jay answered. "This is the first time in months. I have been stopped before during the day, but never at night. But neither do we leave San Marcos very often after dark."

That night Hugo decided to postpone his trip to the city. The road check had unnerved him. He spent a sleepless night, haunted by vivid memories he wanted to forget.

"You go tonight. I'll stay here with the boys," Hugo informed Carmen as Wednesday evening approached. San Marcos seemed the only safe place.

When Jays stopped to pick up their passengers for the evening service, only Carmen was ready. Both boys started screaming when they realized they were being left behind. They wanted Mama. They wanted to ride in Mister Jay's Blazer, not stay home!

Hugo looked at Carmen, threw up his hands, picked up Berton and followed her into the blazer.

Brother Esteban held his audience spellbound with his dynamic preaching, his real-life illustrations, and the loving concern he radiated to the listeners. Hugo knew the words he preached were true. He believed them and longed to have the peace Brother Esteban pleaded with them to receive. But the cost was too great for him. *I've worked my whole life to achieve my self-worth, to be someone of strength. I can't give myself up! The whole village would consider me a weakling.*

On the way home they were again stopped at a road check. Hugo's pulse raced. *Are they looking for me?*

Thursday evening found Carmen and Hugo once again sitting under the voice of Brother Esteban preaching the message of salvation. Conviction raged in Hugo's breast.

"Surrender. Yield yourself to Jesus Christ. Accept him tonight as your personal Saviour. Don't put it off. Behold, today is the day of salvation. You can't run from God. God is everywhere. You can't hide from God. He sees all things and knows all things. 'Whither shall I go from thy spirit? or whither shall I flee from thy presence? If I ascend up into heaven, thou art there: if I make my bed in hell, behold, thou art there. If I take the wings of the morning, and dwell in the uttermost parts of the sea; Even there shall thy hand lead me . . .' Dear friend, all have sinned. I have; you have. 'For all have sinned and come short of the glory of God.'" Brother Esteban paused, his eyes sweeping the audience. "Let us pray."

Earnestly, tenderly he prayed for each one sitting before him. Hugo's heart throbbed painfully, heavily burdened. His sins paraded before him.

Not tonight. He steeled himself to remain seated.

He wouldn't make a fool of himself. The devil patted him on the back. "Wise choice," he whispered. "Christianity is for the weak and foolish."

Hugo's nerves were raw. Sleep had eluded him the past several nights. The unexpected road checks left him shaken. His conscience condemned him. When Jay was again stopped abruptly, this time by barricades across the road, Hugo was certain his time was up. Glinting gun barrels surrounded the Blazer.

Miss Ida sat with her eyes closed, and Hugo knew she was praying. He couldn't move. Time stood still. An eternity passed. He heard nothing, knew nothing, until he felt the Blazer move. In a daze he opened his eyes and knew God had answered whatever prayers Miss Ida had prayed.

"Do you think we should stay home tomorrow night?" Ida asked in a shaky voice.

"No," Jay answered with conviction. "I'm sure it's the work of the devil trying to scare us, not wanting us to hear the teachings of Jesus Christ. Let's sing," he suggested as he reached for his wife's hand, giving it a squeeze of assurance.

"He leadeth me: O blessed thought! O words with heavenly comfort fraught! Whate'er I do, where'er I be, Still 'tis God's hand that leadeth me." They sang softly, their voices harmonizing beautifully. Hugo and Carmen felt God's presence surrounding their gringo neighbors. Where God was, there was no fear.

Chapter 20

Hugo kept his struggles to himself, not seeing the need to share his thoughts with his wife, nor asking if she had questions about the Bible teachings they were receiving each night. He wasn't one to seek another's opinion. He figured out his own way, and expected Carmen to comply readily.

They were entering the dry season which brought cloudless skies and searing heat. Village activity ceased for several hours each afternoon while families sought refuge indoors from the burning sun hanging overhead.

"Be at the phone in ten minutes." Francisco, the young son of the village phone proprietor, gave Hugo his breathless message. "And, mister, she said to tell you it's Vada calling."

Vada! Hugo nearly fell from the hammock where he was taking his siesta. He hadn't thought of his sister for years! Why would she be calling him?

"I'm in the city at Uncle Ian's," his sister explained. "I'm coming out on Monday's bus. Be at

Ameco at four-thirty. Hugo, I'm so excited! It's been years since I've been home!"

Slowly he replaced the receiver. He wasn't too happy with the news. Vada was only a faint memory, and it made him uncomfortable to think of having her around.

"Mister Hugo! Mister Hugo!" It was Francisco again, this time screaming frantically. With each word his panic mounted, until he was speaking gibberish Hugo couldn't understand at all.

"Quiet, calm down!" Hugo commanded sharply, grabbing the boy's shoulders to stop his frenzied dancing. At Hugo's touch the boy collapsed, his head falling back and his eyes rolling upward. He was going into shock. Hugo slapped him.

At that, Francisco's head flew up and he let out a bloodcurdling scream. The slap revived him enough to point to the river. "Red . . . bridge," he gasped.

Francisco's mind was numb from shock. The poor lad could still clearly see his friend leaning over the bridge, teasing a fat sluggish alligator with a stick. Suddenly there was a splash, and his friend slipped beneath the dark water.

Francisco's screaming followed Hugo as he and several other village men raced for the bridge. Nothing disturbed the surface. The water lapped gently against the barrels as it swirled beneath the bridge and flowed down the river. Heavy fronds drooped low over the riverbank, hiding sleeping alligators. No body floated. There was no hint of tragedy.

The men looked at each other. Had something actually happened? They all knew it was useless to explore the river. Huge, dangerous rocks covered the river bottom at the bridge ends. Tons of stone had been dumped at the edges to stabilize the riverbanks for a safe crossing. The murky water of the Ramos River made visibility impossible.

Word spread throughout the village, bringing everyone to the river. Hector, nicknamed Red, wasn't anywhere in the village. Finally Francisco quit crying enough to tell what happened. "We lay like this," the nine-year-old demonstrated as he lay flat on his stomach on the bridge with his head and arms hanging over the water. "We had sticks. Red couldn't reach the biggest alligator, so he got up on his knees at the edge. Then he fell!" Francisco began sobbing for his friend.

"I want Red, I want Red," he screamed.

Men took long poles, probing along the bridge and reaching under it. Several got into dories to give themselves better angles for probing. They found nothing. Defeated, they stopped searching and returned to the village where mourning for Hector had already begun. Screams, wails, and heartbroken weeping filled the street where family and friends milled around Hector's home.

Two occasions brought neighbors together. One

was weddings; the other was death. Today was a day of death.

Young Hector's drowning affected Hugo more than any other death he had witnessed. Life and death were something to be expected. Life brought happiness. Death brought sadness, the loss you felt for the departed. But life continued on after the dead were properly buried. For the first time, Hugo was willing to acknowledge that after one's death, a person faced God. His father, Leo, had. A shudder passed through him. His papa had not even been sober when he met God. Hugo knew he was in no way prepared to face God.

It was a sober little group that gathered at Blanco that Friday evening. The tragedy at San Marcos touched each individual. The death of their own baby son opened fresh wounds in Jay and Ida's hearts. Not one in the group was untouched by sorrow.

"Dearly beloved friends," Brother Esteban opened the service with the comforting words, "Let's pray together before I share what God has laid on my heart.

"Dear Heavenly Father, help each of us gathered here to know with confidence that when our time on earth is finished, we will be gathered home with Thee into the eternal bliss of heaven. Amen.

"My message tonight is on the butterfly. You have beautiful butterflies in your country. My country has some of the same butterflies you have. Others are different, but all are beautiful. This morning I was walking along the jungle surrounding this village. 'Lord,' I prayed, 'what message do you have for me tonight?' Then I saw this butterfly. It was a brilliant purple. It had deep, brilliant purple wings with a black edging. It was striking, and so perfect. I thought to myself, *How can people not believe in God? Only God could create something so incredibly beautiful.* But friends, that butterfly wasn't always beautiful. At one time it was a plain, crawly, fuzzy caterpillar, then a homely pupa. It had to go through *metamorphosis,* or a change in form before it could become beautiful. I have an illustration to help us understand this."

His audience leaned forward, eagerly listening to what he was saying. Butterflies were common, but never had they heard about metamorphosis.

"A butterfly goes through four stages. The egg, the caterpillar, the pupa, and last of all, the adult butterfly. After several weeks of feeding, the caterpillar attaches itself to a branch or other suitable object. It sheds its skin and wraps itself in a pupa. Within this prison, a transformation takes place. The caterpillar structure is developed and feeds the adult structure. Before the adult emerges from the pupa case, the case becomes transparent, revealing the butterfly within. When it emerges as a beautiful adult butterfly, its wings are folded up. By tightening its muscles, it pumps air and blood through its wings, expanding them and allowing them to harden before it can fly.

"We are like butterflies—first a baby, then an innocent child. We reach the pupa stage where our minds are developing, and we know right from wrong. God knocks at our heart's door, bringing conviction to know truth. We search, dissatisfied and wrapped in our ugly prison of self. Finally, we give up self and turn to God for the salvation of our souls. Our past is forgiven and done away with when we repent, when we confess and forsake sin and receive Christ as our personal Lord and Saviour. We feed on God's Word, the Bible. We pray, talking with our heavenly Father, and from that ugly prison of self emerges a new creature. A beautiful soul, clean and unspotted, shining forth the glory of God.

" 'Therefore if any man be in Christ, he is a new creature: old things are passed away; behold, all things are become new.'

"We unfold ourselves to truth. We breathe in the breath of life, feed on God's Word and become strong enough to go forth and share with others the Gospel of salvation."

The picture of man's soul struggling with self, waiting to emerge from its prison, was fixed clearly in the mind of each listener.

Hugo gripped the bench. Condemnation consumed him, but the chains of sin held him fast, and he was powerless to break them.

Saturday Hugo was beside himself with torment. "Mister Jay, you have to do something," he pleaded. "I can't . . . go . . . any . . . longer . . . like . . . this," each word cost him labored effort. So real was his inner battle, that his strength was almost gone.

Tears streamed down Jay's face as he tried to show Hugo the way to peace. "I would gladly ask forgiveness for your sin, Hugo, but I can't. Read with me in Romans 10 verse 9. 'That if thou shalt confess with thy mouth the Lord Jesus, and shalt believe in thine heart that God hath raised him from the dead, thou shalt be saved.' And now verse 13, 'For whosoever shall call upon the name of the Lord shall be saved.'"

Hugo shook his head, unable to speak. It seemed too easy, too sissy. Something held him back. Something stronger than himself.

The believers spent Sunday in prayer for Hugo and Carmen. That evening would be the last night of meetings. As God's Word was preached, the Holy Spirit gently pleaded with Hugo to surrender. The final song was announced. Softly, tenderly the Christians sang:

> I've wandered far away from God,
>   Now I'm coming home;
> The paths of sin too long I've trod, Lord,
>   Lord, I'm coming home.
> Coming home, coming home,

Nevermore to roam,
Open wide Thine arms of love,
Lord, I'm coming home.

Seventeen-year-old Madeline responded to God's call. While she was making her way to the front of the church, her mother rose and followed. She, too, wanted peace.

If two weak ladies have courage to ask forgiveness, a strong man like me should too! Hugo rose from his seat, refusing to listen any longer to the devil's voice urging him not to make a fool of himself.

"Forgive me," he cried in contrition, falling to his knees. "Forgive me. Lord, I believe." His awful burden was lifted, and a glorious peace filled his heart. He rose, unaware that the singing had stopped as the Christians wept with joy. His one thought was for his wife. He wanted her to join him in this decision.

Hugo returned to where his wife was sitting. "Do you understand, Carmen?" he asked her. "Do you understand that my decision to serve Christ is for life? Can you make the same choice? We will serve Jesus Christ for life."

Carmen could only nod. Her heart was too full. If Hugo wanted to believe like Mister Jay and Miss Ida, she wanted to also. Softly the congregation resumed singing:

I've wasted many precious years,
Now I'm coming home;

I now repent with bitter tears,
　　Lord, I'm coming home.
I've tired of sin and straying, Lord,
　　Now I'm coming home;
I'll trust Thy love, believe Thy Word,
　　Lord, I'm coming home.

As they sang, prayers were sent heavenward, interceding for Carmen, that she, too, would join her husband.

"You are sure, Carmen, that you understand?" Hugo asked the second time, wanting her to be fully persuaded. Carmen nodded again, and together husband and wife went forward, seeking forgiveness at the foot of the cross.

For the first time in her life, Carmen's fear vanished and she experienced peace within.

The way home had been long. Why had they fought it? Hugo marveled as the love of God filled him, overflowing to those around him. It was good he couldn't see the gathering storm ahead waiting to test him. Tonight the tropical sky was bright with millions of stars over his serenely sleeping country. No roadblocks stopped their homeward progress. Hugo felt safe, wrapped in divine love.

Chapter 21

Apprehension filled Hugo as Vada alighted from the bus Monday morning. Her bright red lips, glittering earrings, and short skirt looked out of place on someone well in her thirties. Vada's eyes drifted over the crowd gathered at the bus stop. She didn't recognize her just-transformed brother.

Early that morning Hugo had knocked on Mister Jay's door. His clean-shaven face grinned boyishly at his neighbor when he requested, "Could you give me a haircut?"

Hugo's conversion not only changed his heart, but was evident also in his appearance. Now, he had nothing to hide. An open honesty softened his expression. His clean-cut appearance was such a contrast that old acquaintances didn't recognize him.

Vada was dumbfounded when Hugo introduced himself. He didn't even resemble the picture she kept on her fireplace mantel back in Chicago.

"I'm a Christian," Hugo explained to his sister as they returned to San Marcos. He was thankful

Jay had loaned him the mission Blazer, thereby giving him this privacy with his sister.

Vada was furious. Anger flashed from her eyes. "I came to have fun! You won't dare deny me that pleasure! I expect you to take me to the big dance tonight," she demanded, her jaw set in stubborn determination. "Someone on the bus told me to be sure and be there!"

She seethed with anger. She had returned home hoping to find the right man. She expected Hugo to be her confidant. She expected him to introduce her to his circle of acquaintances, giving her an instant advantage. Drink, dancing, and men all played important roles in the wicked lifestyle she led. She wasn't about to be slighted now. Christian? She would see to it that Hugo returned to his senses!

They had barely crossed Ameco's entry and exit *topes* (speed-bumps) when they were stopped by a road check.

"Driver's license and registration," the police demanded.

Hugo reached into his pocket. A look of astonishment crossed his face. "It must be at home. I can't believe I forgot it!" He shook his head in dismay, as he patted first one pocket and then another.

"You'll have to excuse us, mister," Vada interrupted, giving him her most winning smile. Fluttering her eyelashes, she continued, "You see,

I just came from Chicago, and my little brother hasn't seen me since he was about six years old. He was in such a big hurry this morning that he forgot everything but his Blazer!" Vada reached over and rumpled Hugo's hair.

The officer's face relaxed as he leaned forward on the Blazer door. "Always wanted to go to Chicago myself," he admitted. "But you know how hard it is to get a visa."

"Do I ever!" Vada rolled her eyes.

"Enjoy your visit," the officer stepped back and waved them on.

Hugo's conscience smote him. He had told an outright lie. He didn't even have a license anymore. It had been confiscated along with his Toyota. *Why did I say that?*

Kevin and Berton shrank from the strange woman Daddy brought home. They didn't like her. After the first introduction, she ignored them. They were only too glad to escape her loud voice.

Carmen, too, was relieved to turn her back and fry tortillas for dinner. Hugo's older sister made her nervous. She would let her husband entertain her.

When Hugo refused to take her to Monday's dance, Vada turned on him in fury. Curses filled the little house as she ranted and raved, but Hugo would not budge. That evening after Vada left their house for Mama Donado's, Hugo gathered his family together.

"Mister Jay gave me this Bible storybook," he explained as he showed the boys the book filled with pictures. They were thrilled when Daddy promised to read one to them each night before they went to bed.

Hugo's reading sounded like a mockery to his ears. He had lied. He had failed God. As he read he resolved to return to Ameco tomorrow morning and make things right with the police. As soon as he made that decision, his guilt lifted and he felt at peace.

Carmen smiled in contentment. Their sons were snuggled up to their daddy, one on each side, as he read the first story in the book. She had never seen Hugo with short hair, but she liked it. It fit the new Hugo that had been reborn last night.

Mama Donado didn't side with Vada as she had expected. "You leave Hugo alone," Mama said. "Hugo's good. Don't you make trouble for him."

Vada left the house. She would find someone at the tienda to take her. She would show them. She was capable of taking care of herself. Taking her suitcase with her, she found a ride into Ameco to the dance. Instead of returning to San Marcos, she took the first Tuesday bus to the city, not bothering to inform them of her plans.

"I lied to the police yesterday," Hugo confessed to Jay. "Will you take me to Ameco this morning so I can make it right?"

The police officers were speechless when Hugo confessed to them. It was such a little thing!

"Just make sure to get your license before you drive again!" they guffawed, not even asking him his name.

"I need a job," Hugo told Jay on the way home. "Cutting cane for others isn't steady enough, and I don't have any fields of my own."

"We've been praying for you," Jay answered. "One possibility the Lord suggested is woodworking. But it's up to you to decide if you're interested or not. If you are, we are here to help you get started."

The more Hugo thought of making furniture with wood, the more appealing it became to him. Ian had asked him to come work for him in his wood shop in the city. No one in the village did any woodworking except the coffin maker. Woodworking might be the trade to start.

Hugo shared his new plan with his wife. He found communication hard to start with, but Jay had encouraged him to always talk things over with Carmen.

"A husband and wife each need to know what the other is doing and thinking," Jay had admonished. "Don't keep your plans from each other. Share with each other things that happen during the day. Share problems you come across. Talk with each other and pray together."

Hugo was willing. He loved his wife and family

and wanted to be a kind father and husband.

The next day Hugo and Jay went to Ameco to investigate possibilities for selling furniture and purchasing local lumber. They returned home late in the afternoon, well pleased with their venture.

"The men are home! I must go and fix food right away," Carmen cried in dismay. "I don't have anything ready!" She left Miss Ida's in agitation, afraid Hugo would be upset at finding her away from home.

She flew about her kitchen throwing together the flour, shortening, and salt needed to make their supper tortillas. Hugo stuck his head in the door and called out, "Carmen, can you come outside? I'd like to show you something."

Carmen blinked. He hadn't said anything about eating, or why she wasn't home. Her fear faded. Indeed, her Hugo was a different person! She chided herself for forgetting so quickly, and went to see what her husband wanted to show her.

"Jay said it won't take much to fix a work area for me." Hugo's excitement was like a young boy's. "He's going to help me build a roof from this side of the house extending over the back part of our driveway. That will keep the wood dry. We will put up a small shelter for my tools at the end," he exclaimed.

"And Jay will teach me! It's wonderful, Carmen. Now I am anxious to begin work! I will be doing something useful and legal, and, well, it makes me happy, Carmen. Are you happy too?" he asked shyly.

Carmen could only nod. Her heart was too full, but Hugo saw the happiness in her soft, shining eyes and he was satisfied.

Chapter 22

You owe the tortilla factory money because you cheated them, Hugo's conscience spoke, convicting him to make the wrong right. Yes, he had cheated them. At least six hundred dollars worth.

"Lord Jesus, I have no money," Hugo confessed. "But I want to make it right. Help me. Give me courage."

He was thankful for Jay's presence as they went into the factory together to make the wrong right.

The owner listened in amazement at Hugo's confession. "I knew I was cheated, but not who cheated me! Why are you doing this?" he asked.

"My heart is changed," Hugo told him. "I now believe in Jesus Christ. I used to cheat and steal, but I no longer desire to do that. I am a Christian and want to live my life without sin," his voice trembled. It wasn't easy to confess his wrong, but the peace that rested on him for making this right gave him courage.

"Here is one hundred dollars." Hugo handed

the owner the money Jay loaned him. "That is all I have now, but by God's help I will pay the six hundred off before a year is up." They shook hands and the men parted. The owner was impressed by Hugo's commitment. The two brothers in Christ were thankful for God's faithfulness. God blessed Hugo, and before one year was up, he had not only repaid the factory and Jay, but also several other small debts he owed.

"I, too, owe money," Carmen confessed to her husband when he shared his struggle and victory with her. "I borrowed twenty dollars from Elena the time the boys and I took the bus home." Hugo gladly gave her the money and she repaid her debt.

As God reminded the new Christians of incidents that needed correcting, Hugo took care of each one. He returned to Barco and publicly shared his testimony with the villagers. They hated him. Hadn't he used their village to his advantage in his smuggling? This time they didn't even recognize him! But his testimony of what Jesus Christ did for him turned their hate to respect. The change was so evident that they couldn't help believing Hugo's words.

The villagers of San Marcos were uneasy at the change in Hugo. Efran and Vilma's lives changed when they joined the mission church, and the villagers noticed. But Efrans hadn't always lived among them. With Hugo it was different.

The older ones remembered when Hugo was considered the village shrimp. They could recall his turnabout as a teenager, and how he came to be praised and looked up to as the smartest among them. Other men didn't dare cross him. They remembered how he kept to himself, starting and running his business until he owned enough to purchase not one vehicle, but two. After he married, he wasn't seen much. There were rumors that he was one of the top smugglers. Maybe it was true, maybe it wasn't. The villagers didn't know; neither did they ask. "Each man for himself," they believed.

Now Hugo was working at home. He attended the mission church. He dressed differently. He looked different. He acted differently. He used to hang around the church and stare in the windows. Now he openly carried a Bible, sat inside, and sang with the rest.

So great was the change from Hugo's former life that several other villagers visited the mission church. One was Alexandro. Alexandro had labeled Efran as loco after Efran became a Christian. Now that Hugo was a Christian, Alexandro was completely puzzled. One thing he knew, if Hugo was part of this church, they must have something great. Hugo had always chosen the best.

Shy, timid Carmen wasn't one to say much, but if you would have asked her whether her husband had changed, she would have said, "Yes! My Hugo is so different!" And her smile would have convinced you.

If meals were late, he helped her or waited patiently. He learned to talk with her, sharing his thoughts and plans, his joys and disappointments. Kindness was an everyday expression; singing replaced cursing, and prayer came from the heart.

The change in Hugo drew Mama Donado to her stepson's home. She ate many meals with his family. The boys' acceptance of Grandmama, as they happily called her, helped her neglect her bottle. Little by little their love was filling a place in her heart.

Five months of happiness passed, five months of growing closer to God and each other. During weekly instruction classes Hugo and Carmen learned what God wanted for them as His children. Jay was teaching Hugo woodworking. Those five short months passed quickly before their blissful lives faced a frightening interruption.

Chapter 23

"Zing, twang," the saw sang as it bit into the new piece of lumber. Sawdust chips flew steadily through the air, dusting Hugo with a rich mahogany scent.

Hibiscus bushes nodded in the breeze, and birds darted overhead. Kevin and Berton played close by with wood scraps. They were building like Daddy.

Hugo didn't notice the police jeep coming along the street. All his concentration was centered on the board he was sawing for a tabletop. With the board neatly cut in two, he laid down the board and turned off the saw.

The last one, he thought with satisfaction. He couldn't wait to begin sanding the cut edges until they were satin smooth to the touch. He thoroughly enjoyed working with wood, and had put himself wholeheartedly into learning the new trade.

Approaching footsteps caught his attention. He turned, catching sight of the parked vehicle and two officers walking towards him.

"Could you tell us where Hugo Donado lives?" they questioned. Obviously this was the wrong house.

"I am Hugo," he answered quietly. All his previous run-ins with the police flooded back. *This cannot be happening!* he thought. But it was grim reality.

"We have an arrest warrant. You are wanted for questioning," the officer said coldly. His brutal words thrust like daggers through Hugo's heart. His chest tightened, until it seemed his very breath was being wrung from him.

Carmen's gasp from the doorway awakened Hugo. As in a dream he willed himself to walk. *Take a step, now another,* he ordered his feet to obey. Carmen began weeping. Hugo patted her arm awkwardly.

"Tell Jays," he said thickly. Even his tongue wouldn't cooperate. Handcuffs were snapped onto his wrists. He wished the boys were inside. He hated for them to see him like this. He felt the curious stares of the neighbors as they flocked outside their doorways to see what was happening. He saw Jay hurrying over, a look of dismay on his face.

My dear brother Jay, thought Hugo.

"Keep your faith, Hugo. If God is for you, who can be against you?" Jay offered Christ's words of hope. "I'll be right in to see how I can help." Those few heartfelt words gave Hugo courage to walk to the vehicle, not as a beaten man, but as one trusting in an all-knowing, almighty God.

Carmen was shattered. "Come home with us," Ida said gently. "It will make it easier for the boys."

"Why did they take Daddy? Where is he going? When will he be back?" Their perplexing questions tumbled over each other.

"Those are bad men. Daddy's not bad," Kevin staunchly informed Berton. Berton agreed.

"Bad men," he copied.

"Let's have prayer." Jay's words were a healing balm as the little group knelt, pouring out their hearts to God. God was their life. Hugo now believed in Him. The Millers' biggest concern was that Hugo's faith would not waver.

"I'm going to call the brethren in the States before I leave for Ameco. We need to let them know so that they can pray too. Take courage, Sister Carmen," Jay reassured Carmen. "Hugo is in God's hands. And God never leaves His children alone."

Hugo's numbness at the unexpected arrest receded. He was glad for the twenty-five-minute ride. It gave him time to collect his thoughts and pray. When they reached the Ameco jail, Hugo was ready to face whatever lay ahead.

Before becoming a Christian, Hugo had lived a wicked life. He was very thankful he had never killed a man. He wasn't a murderer, in spite of all those years of carrying a knife and gun to protect himself. Many times he had held an enemy at gunpoint, but never had he pulled the trigger or knifed someone.

****

"Six men are being held," Jay told his wife and Carmen when he returned from Ameco. "A Hindu man by the name of Zang turned Hugo in. That much I know, but not what for. I learned little more except that none of them is allowed visitors. I'm going in again tomorrow and will take Hugo his Bible."

The next day Jay was jubilant. "Hugo's Bible passed inspection, and he is allowed to have it in his cell," he said. "The men have been charged with smuggling." He hated to break the news to Carmen.

"He won't get out!" Carmen wept. "He was top man in this district!" Jay and Ida were stunned when Carmen told them the little she knew of Hugo's past. Jay suspected Hugo was far more involved than Carmen had ever been told.

Every day Jay drove to the jail to see if there were any new developments. No one was allowed to visit Hugo or relay any messages. Prayer was the only source of communication the believers had. All were serving the same God who heard their petitions.

Thursday morning, two weeks after Hugo was

arrested, Jay was summoned to the village phone. "Jay, I'm free! Can you believe it? I'm free! Can you come pick me up at the park in Ameco?" Hugo asked.

"Praise God! We'll be right there!" Jay hung up the phone and ran for home.

"Hugo's free! He called and he's free!" Relief, praise, and thanksgiving were all mingled together in his announcement. Carmen hugged the boys. They were thrilled. Daddy was coming home! In minutes they piled in the Blazer, ready to go.

"Daddy!" Both boys pounced on him, barely giving him time to seat himself in the vehicle. The boys' warm welcome was just what he needed after his stay in a cold, metal-and-concrete jail cell.

Thank you, Lord. Thank you. His heart couldn't stop offering thanks for God's mercy to him. His deliverance was miraculous.

"It is a miracle I'm sitting here," Hugo said when the clamor of greetings had subsided. "This morning all six of us were brought into a room and lined up against the wall. I thought my time had come. I honestly never expected to see the outside of prison walls again, yet God gave me calmness and peace. Thank you for bringing my Bible. That is where I found strength and comfort. I laid everything before the Lord. Carmen, you never knew all I was involved in before becoming a Christian. I want to tell you and the Millers sometime, just once, so you understand what God delivered me from, and why it's a miracle I'm sitting here a free . . . a free man . . ." Hugo's voice trailed off. He gazed into the distance, lost in thought.

"Tell us," Jay said.

"Yes." He faced them again. "We were all six lined up against the wall," Hugo continued. "We waited and waited. I don't know how long it was, but it seemed like hours before an officer came in and said, 'Charges have been withdrawn. You are free to go.'

"This morning Zang withdrew charges and refused to show up! I knew I couldn't leave until they understood I had been involved. So I told them. They laughed, 'What's that to us? Get out and never show your face again!'

"My country is full of corruption, Jay. Police, customs, military are all corrupt. You may find it hard to believe, but sadly, it's true," Hugo finished.

"We prayed," Janice reported confidently, her sweet face glowing with an earnest, child-like faith. "Didn't we, Kevin?"

"On the steps we prayed, Daddy, every day," Kevin agreed eagerly. "Now you home," he finished with a happy sigh, wrapping his arms around his beloved father's neck.

Epilogue

Through the cracks in the cornstalk walls, a shaft of sunlight streamed across the kneeling couple at the church front. It seemed to illuminate them with a heavenly glory as they received water baptism.

"Upon the confession of your faith, which you have made before God and these witnesses," the visiting bishop said as he dipped his hands into the basin of water Jay was holding. Cupping up the water, he gently released it over Hugo's head as he solemnly continued, "I baptize you with water in the name of the Father, and of the Son, and of the Holy Ghost." Then taking Hugo by the hand, he said, "In the name of Christ and His church, arise!" As Hugo stood, the saintly, gray-haired bishop looked into his eyes and declared, "And as Christ was raised up by the glory of the Father, even so you also shall walk in newness of life; and as long as you are faithful and abide in the doctrine of His Word, you are His disciple indeed, and shall be acknowledged as a member of the body of Christ and a brother in the church."

With that the bishop brother clasped Hugo's hand, greeting him with the holy kiss. "Brother Hugo, the Lord bless and keep you. Amen."

Joy surged through Hugo. He was now truly a member of the body of Christ and His church. He stood quietly while Carmen was baptized. The bishop's wife came forward to greet her with the holy kiss, welcoming her into the brotherhood of the church.

The little chapel was packed that morning. Many of the villagers filled its benches out of curiosity. Many had witnessed Hugo's handcuffed departure weeks before in the police jeep. They were even more astonished when he returned a free man. His conversion to Christianity intrigued them. As he made his living honestly, working at his trade quietly among them, his example left no question in their minds about his sincerity.

Mama Donado was among the villagers witnessing Carmen and Hugo's baptisms. They had explained their conversion, their repentance from sin, and desire to follow Jesus Christ. She sat subdued, not understanding what had taken place, but knowing that both Hugo and Carmen were different than they had been. She loved the attention they now gave her, and for a fleeting moment she wished she were up front with them. The sunlight falling across the standing couple seemed to come from heaven itself. As Hugo and Carmen turned to face the audience, their faces glowed with happiness, radiating the peace of God that filled their hearts.

Nay, in all these things we are more than conquerors through him that loved us. Romans 8:37

There is no fear in love; but perfect love casteth out fear. 1 John 4:18

Christian Light Publications, Inc., is a non-profit, conservative Mennonite publishing company providing Christ-centered, Biblical literature in a variety of forms including Gospel tracts, books, Sunday school materials, summer Bible school materials, and a full curriculum for Christian day schools and homeschools.

For more information at no obligation or for spiritual help, please write to us at:

Christian Light Publications, Inc.
P. O. Box 1212
Harrisonburg, VA 22801-1212